Click here to claim your free

A sexy prince, an unforgiving enchantement, and a bargain with the fey...

SIGN-UP FOR SAMANTHA'S NEWSLETER AND RECEIVE A *free* EROTIC SHORT STORY!

For my mom, who is nothing like any of the mothers in anything I've written.

AUTHOR'S NOTE

PLEASE NOTE THIS STORY was previously published under the name *Death and Beauty*.

If you have accidentally purchased this story, please contact Samantha MacLeod. She will be happy to offer you another story for no charge!

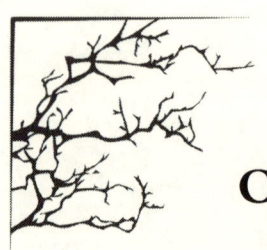

CHAPTER ONE

THE BRANCH TREMBLED, making the delicate green leaves and white flower clusters dance. A single petal shook free to sail across the bright blue sky. It was so beautiful, caught in the golden light of late afternoon. I couldn't understand why someone was crying.

The flower petal tumbled through the sky, heedless of the voices below. I liked it. I liked it all, the bright sky, the white flowers, the audacious little green leaves. I tried to turn and follow the petal through the sky, but my neck wasn't quite working. It didn't matter anyway. Soon the brave little petal would be swallowed by the blackness creeping into my vision, turning the sky into a little, shrinking circle, growing farther and farther away, until it was entirely gone—

Darkness. Darkness and voices, a soft rush of motion. Then something harsh and acrid, like battlefield smoke, stung my nostrils, and my head spun. I tried to open my eyes.

"What happened?" I moaned.

Someone clucked above me. "Don't move just yet, my boy."

The voice sounded old and only mildly sympathetic. I ignored it, pushing myself up to sitting. My head throbbed and my stomach surged, making me gag. Soft hands grabbed my arm, dragging me back to the bed. Her grip felt weak, but I didn't have the strength to resist.

"Where am I?" I whispered, once my stomach stopped roiling.

"You're dead, dearie."

I shook my head, making the room spin. "No. That's not possible."

She clucked again. My eyes were adjusting to the gloom, and I could just make out a hunched figure tending to a fire. "Oh, that's what they all say."

HEL'S LOVER 3

"No, you don't understand. I'm—"

"Baldr the Beautiful," she said. "Óðinn's favorite son. Yes, yes, we know all about you here."

"But I can't die. My mother is Frigg. She traveled the Nine Realms, and everything she found—"

"Promised not to harm you. I know. I heard all about it."

The old woman turned and gave me a sympathetic, tired smile. She looked like a nice woman, but of course you never can tell. "But your mother couldn't possibly have gotten a promise from every single thing."

She hobbled a bit closer to the bed, her arms outstretched with a rough wooden bowl in her hands. "Drink this, dearie. It'll help."

I tried to push myself up to sitting. Again, my head and stomach revolted, throbbing and churning. The old woman chuckled sympathetically.

"It takes some getting used to, being dead," she said. "Tell you what, Baldr the Beautiful. Why don't we talk about the last thing you remember, hmmm?"

I clenched my hand into a fist, momentarily fighting the urge to punch her. But I was clearly in no shape for punching anything and, in my experience, punching rarely improved the situation. So I tried to remember. My mind was strangely clouded and unhinged, as if I'd had too much mead.

"Ah. Right." I opened my eyes, blinking at the rough wooden beams above me. "We were playing a game…"

It was a game, I guess, although I'd grown tired of it by that point. After my mother made every single thing in the Nine Realms pledge not to harm me, I turned invulnerable. Which was, admittedly, rather helpful. The game started innocently enough, in the small hours of the night, celebrating another magnificent battle. Someone dropped a dagger, someone else accidentally kicked it, and the dagger ended up in one of Val-Hall's hearthfires. I reached in and grabbed it; flame, steel, and ash wood had all vowed not to harm me, so I was fine.

Well. That was the beginning of the end. The whole crowd went wild and, before I fully realized what was happening, I was dragged outside and pelted with everything the drunken crowds of heroic warriors could imagine. Yup, iron didn't hurt me. Neither did stone. Arrows bounced right off my chest. Same with burning pitch.

Hilarious, right?

I thought the fervor would die down. No such luck. A day or so later, all the Æsir wanted in on the fun. Even my own brother Thor tossed his magical hammer at me. I was scared enough to duck, although of course it didn't touch me. And then Höðr, my blind brother, threw something tiny in my direction...

I gasped. Pain. I remembered a blinding flash of bright white pain, and the sudden shock of betrayal. A flash of white against the blinding blue sky. Then darkness.

"Yes, you've remembered it, then. Won't do to dwell on it now, Baldr." The woman patted my arm.

"But that's impossible! I'm Baldr. I'm invulnerable."

She clucked again. "Oh yes, your mother Frigg traveled the Nine Realms, forcing a promise not to harm you from everyone. And almost everything."

I groaned. "Almost. What happened?"

"Mistletoe, dearie. Innocent little mistletoe. There's always an exception, is there not?"

She shook her head and wrapped a surprisingly strong arm around my back, helping me sit. My head and stomach had calmed some, and the steaming, golden liquid in that wooden bowl didn't look half bad. She raised it to my lips and I took a sip. It was good, hot and salty.

"I've got a son," I whispered as she lowered the bowl.

"Mmmm, yes. Forsetti. Fully grown, that one. But yes, he will mourn you."

My son, Forsetti Baldrsen. True, he was fully grown and happily married. But now I wouldn't get to meet my own grandchildren? Pain lanced through me like fire.

"I'm married," I pleaded.

"Not anymore," she said. "Death breaks all bonds."

Well, shit. I sank back on the bed, exhausted. Death breaks all bonds, huh? I wondered how Nanna would feel about that. She was a good wife, I suppose, although I often wondered if she'd ever actually wanted to be married to me.

She told me once she cried with happiness when her parents said she'd been betrothed to Baldr the Beautiful. I'm almost certain that was the last time I brought her so much joy. She loved going to parties together, chatting with her friends while their jealous eyes watched my every move. Or cheering for me from the stands as I sang one of Bragi's epic ballads. But when it came to actually spending time with me, sharing a meal or a conversation or even occasionally spreading her legs, I always had the lingering feeling she'd rather be elsewhere. That she'd married the Beautiful, not the Baldr.

Or perhaps I only told myself that to assuage my guilt. There were thousands of women in the Nine Realms, and they were all drawn to me. Resisting every single one proved to be too much of a challenge. Rather frequently, in fact.

But still.

"I've got to get back," I said. "How do I get back?"

The old woman groaned in disapproval. "Ah, Baldr. Such a pity."

I frowned. "What?"

"You know, you're the first true Æsir to actually die. And yet you're just asking the same questions as everyone else. I expected better."

"Then who's in charge here?" I asked, struggling to keep my eyes open. "I've got to talk to who's in charge."

"All in good time, dearie. You've nothing but time now, you know."

I tried to speak, but my words were swallowed by exhaustion. I sank into blackness.

WHEN I WOKE, THE OLD woman was gone and I was alone in a small, round hut. The fire had gone out, but I didn't feel cold. I threw off the blanket, sat up, and pulled my rough linen shirt over my head, running my fingers over my breastbone, feeling for injuries. Everything felt normal, but it still took me a minute to find the courage to look down.

My chest was fine. No wounds, no holes, no scars. Thank the Nine Realms.

I didn't recognize either the shirt or the soft leather pants I wore, and for a moment I wondered if I'd been put on my funeral pyre in such ordinary clothes.

No. Óðinn would never let his favored son go out of Asgard looking like this. Knowing my father, he'd turn my funeral into another occasion to impress his friends and terrify his enemies. A real spectacle of might and power.

I groaned and stretched, heading for the hide-covered door. A strange blue light filled the hut when I pulled the door aside, blinding me. Once my eyes adjusted I saw a dark, jagged mountain range in the distance. Blue-green foothills sloped toward me, meeting a wide, sparkling river. A haphazard scattering of huts sprinkled the rolling hills between me and the river. People moved among the huts, working in gardens or leaning against walls, chatting. The scent of baking bread drifted across the peaceful valley. I rubbed my eyes and looked again. It wasn't exactly what I expected for Niflhel, the realm of the inglorious dead.

Inglorious. That stung, but I hadn't fallen in battle, had I?

I swallowed the growing lump in my throat and set off, walking down the hill and toward the closest person I could see, a young woman picking herbs in a small, fenced garden.

"Hello?" I said.

"Oh!" She jumped and stood. Once she saw me her cheeks flushed and she smiled shyly, brushing back her hair.

Ah. I guess I still looked like myself, then.

"Hello!" she said. "Are you new?"

"Yeah, I guess I am. I'm just wondering who's in charge?"

She giggled, although I hadn't meant that as a joke, and the flush across her cheeks deepened.

"I mean, I'd like to know how all this works?" I pressed.

"Oh! You just, you know, you just do what you'd like," she stammered. "You do what pleases you." She covered her smile with her hand.

Great. I was getting exactly nowhere with her.

"Thank you," I said, giving her my most winning smile as I turned to leave.

"Unless you were talking about Hel?" Her expression dropped.

"Hel?" I asked. The name rang a distant bell, but my mind was still irritatingly clouded and I couldn't quite grasp the association.

She frowned. "She's in charge, I guess. I only saw her once, but..." Her voice trailed off and she shivered.

"Thank you! And where do I find Hel?"

"She's up the river, in the castle. I don't think you'll get much from her, though. No one ever does. And, you know, it's not bad here."

I rubbed the back of my neck, glancing around. The door to her hut was ajar, showing a large sleeping platform and a pair of men's boots just inside the doorframe.

"Did you and your husband, uh, pass on together?" I asked.

Her eyes widened. "Oh, no! Nothing like that. We found each other here. Although I should tell you, people don't like to talk about their lives before. It's kind of, uh, rude."

I thanked her kindly for the advice and walked toward the river. I'd gone about ten steps when someone called my name.

"Baldr! Stop right there, Baldr!"

I turned back and saw the old woman hurrying down the path.

"Oh, no you don't," she said, panting, as she reached me. "Don't go running off on your doula like that!"

"Doula?" The term was unfamiliar to me.

"That's me. I assist the passage. And I'm not done assisting. You're just up a bit earlier than expected, my boy."

I returned her smile. "I didn't realize I needed assistance."

She cackled. "Well, now, of course you didn't. And you don't need much, really. I just wouldn't want you wandering off into the darkness before you've even had a chance here."

"The darkness?"

The old woman raised an eyebrow. "See? Now it's a good thing you still have me. Let's get back to the house, I've food for you."

THE STONE HUT SEEMED even smaller than I remembered. I crouched on the bed, my head stooped to avoid hitting the roof beams, while the old woman unwrapped a package of fresh cinnamon rolls. I was surprised when my stomach rumbled at their spicy honeyed scent.

"You don't have to eat, of course," she said, handing me a roll. "Your body doesn't need it anymore. But eating's always been about more than just fuel."

"These are amazing," I said, around a mouthful of cinnamon bun.

She nodded. "That they are. It's Lucy just down to road who bakes them."

I chewed while I tried to wrap my head around that one. "So...people still work, then?"

"Well, people find something to do. Most people, that is. I don't know if Lucy was a baker before, mind you. Ah, and I should warn you not to talk too much about what came before. It's—"

"Rude," I finished. "Yes, I heard." I wiped my fingers on my pants and looked out the door. The strange blue light was stronger now, shimmering off the distant mountains and turning the river to a shining band of silver light. *Up the river, in the castle.* That's what the girl said when I asked where to find Hel.

"What's past the river?" I asked. "In the mountains?"

A shadow passed over the old woman's face. "Ah, yes. That's the darkness, boy. That's where you go when you've had enough here. When you're ready for what comes next."

I nodded as if that statement made sense. "And what's up the river?"

She cackled again. "Oh, clever, clever, Baldr the Beautiful! Yes, that's where Hel governs her realm. But you won't get anything out of her, dearie. No one ever does."

I shrugged. "No one mortal, you mean. Didn't you say I'm the first Æsir to come here?"

Her wrinkled face broke into a wide grin. "That's my boy. Here, let me pack you another cinnamon roll. You tell the guards old Ada says hello."

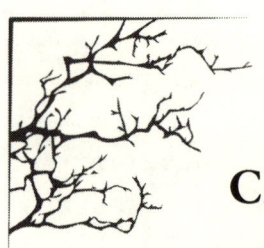

CHAPTER TWO

IT TOOK ME TWO DAYS to reach the castle, although I could have covered the distance faster if I hadn't been constantly distracted by the landscape and the changes in my own body. It was disconcerting to not grow hungry and, although my body was tired by the end of the day, I didn't feel like I actually needed sleep. I stopped at night anyway, trying to find somewhere comfortable to lie down and watch the unfamiliar constellations whirl in the darkness above me.

And I tried very hard not to worry about what would happen to the Nine Realms without me serving as Óðinn's diplomat.

Although the sun at midday was almost indistinguishable from Asgard, dawn and dusk in Niflhel were decidedly blue. The evening sky was fading from bright cerulean to a darker cobalt when I first saw the brooding towers of Hel's citadel. By the time I reached the iron gates, the sun had set and the sky was a wash of indigo. Orange torches burned on pikes; the enormous gates stood wide open and unguarded.

I approached slowly, expecting to be stopped. Not even Óðinn's Val-Hall was unattended. But no one stood at attention inside the gates, so I walked under the wide arch, more uneasy than I would have been willing to admit.

Voices drifted through the open air and lights flickered in many of the windows. The entire castle was made of dark, reflective stone cut to harsh angles, making a strange backdrop for cheerful voices and the smell of roasting meat. My mouth watered. Even if I didn't need to eat anymore, damn, I could go for some roast beef and a flagon of mead.

The first guard was just inside the castle doors, a portly, middle aged man sitting in a large armchair. Oddly, he appeared to be tuning a lute. He gave me a cheerful smile.

"Excuse me, good sir," I said, with a small bow. It never hurts to be polite. "Is this where I may find the Lady Hel?"

He laughed. "You must be new here."

I admitted that was indeed the case, and asked again where I may find Mistress Hel.

"Just through that door," he said, pointing with the neck of his lute. "But, for Asgard's sake, don't call her Lady. Or Mistress."

"What title does she prefer?"

He snorted. "Honestly, I think she prefers to be left alone."

"Oh. Well, thank you for your time, sir."

He raised an eyebrow. "You do know what you're looking for, right?"

My smile faltered. Something danced along the edges of my mind, some information about Hel Lokisdóttir I'd heard and had managed to forget. I'd been trying to recall all the stories about Niflhel as I walked, but most of them stayed maddeningly out of reach. I guess I'd always assumed the realm of the inglorious dead would never apply to Baldr the Beautiful.

"Yes, I believe I do," I said. I shouldn't be overconfident, but showing weakness was risky too. This casual atmosphere could be a trap. It wouldn't have taken an espionage expert to see me coming and prepare a ruse.

He shrugged and went back to his lute. "Well, good luck to you."

I turned down the hall, walking in the direction he'd indicated. After a few paces, I opened a set of oaken doors and found a feast hall.

It looked like the main room in Val-Hall, although the ceilings were higher and the walls darker. The room was stuffed with men and women at long, food-laden tables. A small band wandered through the chaos, singing ballads I only half recognized, and everyone was cheering and toasting. They all seemed pretty damn drunk. If this was part of a trap, it was bizarrely elaborate.

I stopped a few of the revelers and asked for Hel. Most of them laughed in my face or clapped me on the back. All of them offered me mead, which I declined as politely as possible. One of the musicians finally took pity on me and pointed me toward a dark hallway.

"She's usually in her study, this time of night," the young woman said. She had wine-flushed cheeks and a beautiful singing voice.

"My thanks," I said.

Her cheeks grew brighter as she dropped a quick glance down my unbuttoned collar. "Hurry back," she said.

I gave her a smile that could mean whatever she wanted it to mean and left the feast hall.

A LONG RECTANGLE OF golden light spilled across the darkened hallway. I walked toward it, the echo of my own footsteps growing as the noise of music and feasting faded behind me. Slowly I became aware of a different set of voices. I stopped and held my breath, listening.

"—reports that new arrivals have slowed somewhat, at least in the Northern corner. And travelers to the darkness are holding steady." It was a man's voice, nasal and droning.

"Thank you." That was a woman. Her full, rich voice practically rippled with authority. "And the East?"

"Certainly, your Majesty!" Another woman, this one younger and excited. "Arrivals are steady there as well. This year's harvest must be holding."

"Wait. Ganglati, we have a visitor."

The voices fell silent, replaced by the soft rustle of clothing and scuff of shoes against stone. I blinked as a light swung into the hallway.

"Yes?" It was the man with the nasal voice. He was tall and thin, with a prominent nose and full lips. He held a lantern.

I raised my hands in front of my chest to show I had no weapons and gave him a broad, easy smile. "I beg your pardon, good sir. I'm seeking the Lady Hel."

His face scarcely moved, but I sensed a strange interplay of repressed expressions. Amusement, perhaps?

"Let him enter." The woman's voice spoke from behind him.

"Very well," he said, bowing to the side.

I thanked him and walked through the door. The room was sparsely furnished, with a low hearthfire and a large table. A severe black chair dominated the far end of the room.

On the chair sat a skeleton.

A moving skeleton.

I pressed my lips together and held my back stiff, fighting the urge to scream. My hands moved to my hip, feeling for the greatsword I'd carried most of my life. It was not comforting to remember I was completely unarmed.

An enormous blue eyeball jerked in the skeleton's head as it examined a ream of parchment on the table, its bony fingers flicking through the pages. The skeleton's lower jaw moved, and the woman's rich voice echoed across the room.

"One moment."

The room was silent as she turned the parchment with a dry rustle. After flipping over the last page, she sighed and turned toward me. Only my decades of warrior's training with Óðinn kept me from running.

She wasn't a skeleton.

She was *half* a skeleton.

The right side of her face and body was a young woman with pale skin and dark hair, wearing a utilitarian brown dress. And the left side of her body was a corpse. As I stared, something sleek and dark shifted inside her exposed rib cage, disrupting the tatters of her dress. I was suddenly very grateful I'd not eaten anything at that feast.

"You've found me," the skeleton woman said. "What do you want?"

I swallowed hard against the bile rising in my throat. "Gracious Lady, my name is—"

"Stop." The bones of her fingers clattered as she waved her hand in the air. "Stop it. I know who you are, Baldr Óðinnsen. And I can guess why you're here."

"Oh, really?" I gave her my most winning smile.

It was met with a flat stare from both her living and her dead eyes. "Let me guess. You've come to offer me your heroic assistance, anything I desire, in exchange for one tiny, little favor."

I tried to widen my smile. "Perhaps, dear Lady."

She snorted. "Stop. Please, by the Nine Realms. It's just Hel. And am I on the right track, Baldr?"

"You are most perceptive," I admitted.

"So you've come to request a boon. And what did you have in mind as an exchange, son of Óðinn? Were you going to offer to ride out against my enemies? To defend my borders? To act as my champion in single combat?"

I bowed so low I was almost even with her feet, one clad in a simple sandal and one made of bone. With, if I wasn't mistaken, a single maggot in the ankle. I tried to concentrate on the foot with the sandal.

"I would consider it my honor and my duty, my...uh. Hel."

She laughed. Her voice rang out, bouncing off the walls and growing in strength. I frowned as I stood. Her attendants were laughing too. The tall, thin man at least had the dignity to attempt to cover his mouth, but the young women were laughing openly.

"I...I'm not sure I understand," I said.

Hel wiped her living eye with her skeletal hand. "Oh, you fool. We're dead! What borders do we have to defend, Baldr Óðinnsen? Niflhel echoes the world above, and it belongs to only us! What enemies do the dead have?"

She stood. The effect was quite disconcerting; I could see her femur rotating in her pelvis.

"And why would I need a champion? Who would dare to attack me?"

I swallowed, thinking fast. "Let me teach you."

Her living face raised an eyebrow. "You? Teach me?"

"Of course! What do the rest of the Nine Realms have that Niflhel lacks? Just knowledge, my Lady—I mean, Hel."

She turned, examining me with the skeletal eye. I suppressed a shiver.

"You think I lack knowledge?" Her voice was hard as steel.

I forced myself to smile. "Don't we all have something to learn?"

Several of her attendants laughed, but I ignored them and focused all my attention on Hel. She'd turned so all I could see was her decaying skeletal visage. With no face or skin, it was impossible to read her expression. I had no way of knowing if my smile, or my unbuttoned shirt, was having any effect.

I had the sinking feeling it wasn't.

Hel faced me again and a cold, thin smile crept across her living lips. "Very well, Baldr, son of Óðinn. I'll offer you a deal."

A low murmur spread through the crowd of attendants. It did nothing to make me feel more comfortable.

"You teach me something I don't already know," she said, "and I'll grant you one boon. Anything you ask."

There was a gasp at that, quickly hushed. I frowned.

"You'll have three days," Hel said. "Beginning at sunrise. Now, Eriksen, please show our new guest to his quarters."

My mind spun as the tall, thin man led me from the room.

What in the Nine Realms had I just agreed to do?

CHAPTER THREE

THE KNOCK CAME JUST after sunrise. I'd spent the night tossing and turning in my sumptuous guest suite, until I finally abandoned the bed to pace the floor and wish I'd paid more attention to Óðinn's lessons about... well, about everything.

"Come in," I said, expecting one of the attendants from last night.

The door swung open with a little gust of cool air. I glanced up and jumped. Hel stood in the doorway, her dark hair pulled back in a tight ponytail, her living arm and her dead arm crossed over a dark blue dress with a modest, unflattering cut.

"Good morning, Óðinnsen. I trust the accommodations are suitable?"

"Of course," I said, forcing a smile.

"Would you care to join me for breakfast? I assume you want to begin instructing me as soon as possible."

Her living eye sparkled at that, but her face remained impassive. My stomach shifted uncomfortably. I couldn't tell if she was mocking me.

"Breakfast would be lovely," I said.

She turned from the room and I followed, my steps matching hers.

"As for the, uh, instruction. What topic interests you the most?"

She laughed once, a sharp, harsh bark. "Oh, no you don't, Baldr. You don't get off that easily."

That shut me up. I followed her through what felt like miles of dark stone corridors in silence, my apprehension growing stronger with each step.

I had to get out of here. The realm of the inglorious dead wasn't bad, from what I could tell, but this was not where I belonged. I needed to get back to Asgard. The Æsir would tear themselves apart without me. They were a catty, argumentative group even when times were good. Óðinn and Frigg needed me to smooth over hurt feelings, to make everyone smile and laugh.

I was useless here in Niflhel.

Hel stopped so abruptly I almost walked into her. She hesitated before a tall set of polished, black doors. For a heartbeat, it almost looked as if she were smiling. Then the doors swung open, and my heart sank.

We stepped together into the largest library I'd ever seen. Bookshelves lined the walls, soaring far above my head. Each shelf housed its own ladder, perched on wheels and ready to slide across the room.

Shit.

Hel strode across the room, pointedly ignoring my reaction, and sat at a little table tucked under a window. Two steaming mugs waited on the dark surface. She crossed her legs and rested her face on her coiled, skeletal hand.

I joined her, making myself smile. The living side of her face was almost as blank and expressionless as the dead side; it was impossible for me to get a read on her. Was she hoping to intimidate me? Was this all as an elaborate joke?

That made me shiver. Her father was Loki the Lie-smith, after all. I didn't think they were close, but you never knew. He could have taught her quite a bit.

"That's a lot of books," I said, trying to sound casual as I reached for my mug.

She shrugged. Maybe she was amused, or maybe she was bored.

"You've read them all?" I asked.

I meant it as a joke, but she responded with a prim nod. "Of course. As you said, the only thing the other Realms have on Niflhel is knowledge."

I winced, then glanced up, hoping she hadn't noticed my reaction. Luckily, she was staring out the window.

"Fascinating things going on in Greece," she said, almost to herself.

"Greece?" I asked.

She looked directly at me for the first time. Her large, pale eye rotated in the empty socket.

"We trade books," Hel said. "The Lord of their Underworld and I. We have an agreement."

"Oh," I stammered. I didn't even know there was more than one underworld.

"Ah, here comes breakfast," said Hel. "You prefer smoked fish, do you not?"

I nodded miserably. I couldn't name a single thing Hel enjoyed, or didn't enjoy, and she already knew what I liked for breakfast.

I was totally screwed.

AFTER BREAKFAST, WE walked together through the grounds of her palace, shared lunch in a pavilion overlooking the river, and then spent the afternoon touring her orchards. Hel's palace was nothing like I'd expected, and about as far from Óðinn's Val-Hall as I could imagine. Everyone in the castle, she said, was here by choice. The feast ran constantly but, unlike my father's realm, Hel expected nothing from the people eating, sleeping, and partying in her castle. Some of the servants, she admitted late in the afternoon, were probably hoping to curry favor with her. And they were free to leave once they realized it wouldn't work.

Great, I told myself. I'm sure that little comment had absolutely nothing to do with me.

Hel saved the orchards for last, and she said very little about them. She walked on my right side, showing me none of her living body. I offered her every piece of wisdom, advice, folklore, and rumor I could possibly remember, and all I got was an occasional nod or, even worse, a contemptuous snort. I'd never met a woman more immune to my charms, and she grew even more cold and distant the moment we stepped under the flowering branches of her extensive orchards.

This place meant something to her, then.

But I had no idea what.

THE SECOND DAY DID nothing to alleviate my sense of impending doom.

Hel offered to take me on a tour of Niflhel in her chariot. Of course, she was an expert charioteer. We rode along the river through low, rolling hillsides dotted with chest-high red clay cones. I watched them for a long time before finally realizing what they were.

"Beehives," I said.

Hel raised an eyebrow. "Indeed. Please tell me you didn't think I'd be surprised by that?"

I laughed. "Of course not. Do you know what you can make with honey?"

"I know at least thirty uses for honey," she said, her voice level. "And yes, I do realize that's how you make mead."

My heart sank. Again. We rounded a gentle corner and a herd of sheep scattered before the stallion pulling our chariot, bleating their displeasure as we trotted past. Sheep. Hey, I did know something interesting about sheep!

"Hel, did you know you can collect a waxy oil from sheep and use it to—"

"Waterproof clothing?" she finished. "Or as a remedy for dry skin? It's useful to breastfeeding mothers as well."

I threw my hands up. "Why in the Nine Realms do you know so damned much about sheep?"

She met my gaze. Her face remained stoic, but I got the distinct feeling she was amused. "Should I rule and know nothing of my kingdom? What if someone came to me with a question I could not answer? What would that make me?"

I shrugged. "Normal?"

Hel turned, showing me her skeletal side. I had the sneaking suspicion that was Hel's way of avoiding any display of emotion. Something I'd said must have affected her, but I had no idea if she was amused or irritated.

After a long silence, Hel turned the chariot and we peeled away from the river, following the meanders of a small tributary. The hills grew close and the trail narrowed until there was barely enough room for the chariot to pass. Then the landscape spread out again, and we entered a strangely beautiful valley.

Tall stalks of pale flowers waved in the breeze, their movements echoing the dance of slender birch trees across the valley. Our chariot pushed through the flowers, and the blossom-laden stalks parted like waves before us.

Hel stopped the chariot at the foot of the birch trees. Without a word, she unhooked the stallion's harness, patted him on the nose, and let him graze.

"Aren't you worried he'll run off?" I asked.

"No," she said. "Get out."

I did as she said. "Are you leaving me here?"

Hel raised her eyebrow, then unfastened a clasp and opened the chariot's seat, revealing a small woven bag and a large white blanket. I followed her as she spread the blanket under the trees.

"What's this?" I asked.

"Lunch." The ghost of a smile played across the living side of her face. I wondered if she'd taken anyone else to this meadow. Doubtful. I couldn't imagine too many of the dead would want to ride next to her rotting, skeletal half.

Although she didn't look so terrifying now, sitting on a white blanket and holding a strange oval-shaped fruit. She pulled a small blade from the bag and started peeling the fruit, revealing soft flesh the color of sunrise.

"Nice place," I said, watching her.

She murmured in agreement.

"What are those flowers? The white ones?"

"Asphodel," she said. "I only planted one, and now they've filled the entire valley."

I glanced out at the sea of white blossoms. "You planted those?"

She turned away, showing me the bones and tendons of her left side. I whistled, trying to imagine how long it would take one flower to seed this entire valley. And how many lonely trips she must have made during that time, watching the flowers spread.

"Thank you," I said, sitting down on the blanket. The tall, pale flowers seemed even more impressive from the ground. "I may not know a damn thing you don't already know, but I'm glad I saw this."

Her ribcage shook as she exhaled and I turned away, not wanting to make her feel uncomfortable. After all, I might have been totally wrong about this valley. Maybe she brings people here all the damn time.

"It's a thin place," she said, finally.

I turned back to see her cut a sliver of orange fruit and lean down, closing her lips around it. I watched as she chewed. I should have been able to see the bright flash of orange fruit through her skull, but I couldn't. Odd.

"What do you mean?" I asked.

"The darkness is just through those trees," she said, nodding behind me. "Most people think you need to cross the river to find it, but it's here."

That raised the hairs on the back of my neck. I reached for my waist, where I'd always carried my greatsword, and turned to follow her gaze.

Nothing but silver birch trees, swaying in the breeze. Light flashed and shimmered off their pale green leaves.

"I don't see anything," I said.

She laughed, although it sounded almost like a sigh. "No. You only find the darkness when you're looking for it. Or when it starts to call for you."

I shivered. "What is it?"

She speared another sliver of fruit on her silver knife and offered it to me. "It's what comes next. Where you go when you're done with here."

I took the fruit, surprised at how slippery it felt between my fingers. The flavor was exquisite, honeyed sweetness with an unexpected tang that almost brought tears to my eyes. I licked my fingers, not caring if I was being rude.

"That's delicious."

Hel turned away again, her shoulder bone shivering. "Thanks."

"You still haven't answered my question. What is the darkness? What comes next?"

Her exposed collarbone shrugged. "Some say you simply vanish, like smoke. Others say you re-enter the world, starting all over again in a new body, wiped clean of your memories."

Hel was staring into the forest, showing me the back of her head. The dark hair of her living half had worked its way out of her braid to blow in long waves across her pale skull. I had the momentary, foolish urge to catch her hair and tuck it behind her ear.

"Does it call to you?" I asked in a whisper.

She laughed, a harsh, bitter bark. "Of course not," she said, smoothing her dress over her knees as she turned back to the asphodel field. "I'm ruler of this realm. I can't leave."

I grinned at her. "Sure you can leave. That's one of the perks of being ruler, right? You can do whatever you want."

Hel gave me a severe frown. "Are you suggesting I abdicate?"

I shrugged. "I'm not suggesting anything. But I suspect there's, oh, at least a dozen people back there in your castle who'd be willing to take on the whole ruler position."

I thought she might be angry at that, but she sighed instead, turning the half-peeled fruit over in her hands. "Perhaps. But...I don't think any of them would be as good at it."

That made me laugh. She frowned, both her blue eyes once again shooting daggers at me.

"What's so funny?" she demanded.

"Oh, nothing. It's just, we've got something in common."

She scowled and straightened her back. "I have nothing in common with you, Baldr the Beautiful."

"But you do. Because that's just what I was thinking this morning. That's why I've got to get back to Asgard. No one else can do what I do."

She turned away. I saw her skeletal teeth grind together. "And what is it you do?"

"I keep them all from killing each other." I sighed. "I'm basically Baldr the Babysitter."

I took a deep breath before I turned to gauge her reaction. I'd felt like a babysitter for a long time in the echoing halls of the Æsir, but I hadn't dared share my feeling with anyone. It wouldn't look good for Óðinn's favorite son to whine.

Hel gave me a fragile smile before she turned to unpack delicate meat-filled pastries and a wooden bowl of shredded carrot salad. She ate very little, said nothing at all, and spent most of the meal turned away from me, watching the trees in the forest. I guessed the darkness was calling to her pretty strongly, and I couldn't understand why that thought should bother me. If she wandered off into those trees, maybe I'd be free to go back to Asgard.

I finished my second pastry and stood, wiping my hands on my pants. "I'll be right back," I said. "Don't leave."

My tone was fiercer than I'd intended, and she met my eyes with a flicker of surprise before giving me a silent nod. I wandered around the chariot to take a leak. The elaborately carved seat caught my eye as I walked back. There was another, much larger clasp on the far side.

"Hel!" I called.

"I'm here," she said. I turned to see her come to her feet, pulling the blanket off the grass.

"What's in the seat?"

She shrugged. "Hunting gear. Sparring equipment."

Hunting gear. I flipped the clasp, opened the seat, and grinned. There were a pair of bows, two quivers, several swords, and a dozen small daggers.

"Oh, Hel," I said. "I think I know something I can teach you."

I SET UP THE FIRST target at the base of the birch trees. Hel let me use the white blanket, which I folded over twice and propped against a thick trunk to make a target which would be small but hopefully not impossible to hit. By the time I got back to the chariot, Hel was watching me with a slightly unnerving gleam in her eyes.

"Archery," I said, handing her a bow and a single arrow before turning back to the chariot to dig out the full quiver. We'd be losing some arrows today for sure. "I'll show you how to string it, and then—"

The bowstring twanged, followed almost immediately by a solid thwack.

Shit.

I looked at the target first. The arrow I'd just handed Hel trembled against the birch trunk. It was embedded solidly in the center of the white blanket.

"Oh, come on!" I cried. "When were you going to tell me you could shoot?"

Her eyes danced. "Maybe you're a better shot," she said, handing me the bow.

I tugged the bowstring. This wasn't a great bow and, honestly, it had been a while since I'd practiced archery. Still. I had to be better than an animate skeleton, right? I notched the arrow and held my breath as I pulled back the string. *Twang.* My shot went wide, the arrow skidding past the tree and well into the forest.

"Damn," I muttered. "I think the balance on that arrow was off."

Hel's lip twitched. It looked like she was fighting a smile.

"Go ahead and gloat," I said, handing her the bow. "You're clearly a better shot. But now, let's try swords."

"SHIT," I HISSED.

I was out of breath, and out of ideas. The point of Hel's dark blade hovered inches from my exposed throat.

By all Nine fucking Realms, Hel was an expert swordsman. No one had ever disarmed me that quickly. I didn't know what hurt more, the hand she'd hit with the broad end of that black hunting sword, or my damaged pride.

She'd beaten me again, and now she had me pinned against a tree trunk. Her eyes flashed and the loose strands of her hair fluttered around her neck, looking almost golden in the bright sunlight.

"What's next, Baldr?" she asked, arching an eyebrow at me.

"Give me a minute," I panted, holding my hands up in surrender. "You win with the swords."

I almost missed her response. If I'd been a second faster to bend down and reclaim my sword from the trampled grass, I wouldn't have seen her smile.

That smile. I froze halfway to the ground, staring at her. For the first time since I met her, Hel actually looked happy. But it was more than that; she looked different. Her face was flushed with color, and her pale eyes sparkled.

She looked beautiful.

It may have been a trick of the light, or my exhaustion, or just my embarrassment at being beaten so handily by a woman. But still, for a heartbeat, the fearsome ruler of Niflhel looked beautiful.

She caught my eye and her expression changed, her smile vanishing as her back stiffened. She turned away quickly, and I was again staring at her exposed shoulder blade.

"I'm sorry," I stammered. "I didn't mean to—"

"It's nothing," she said, her voice once again cold and distant. "Let's go."

I picked up the sword, wiped the blade across my pants, and sheathed it before following Hel into the chariot. She was silent as I packed up the swords, bows, and arrows. I felt a pang of regret as I closed the clasp on the weapons, although I couldn't for the life of me explain why.

"What do you have to teach me next, Baldr?" The sharp edge to her voice was unmistakable, and I wondered what the hell I'd just done to piss her off so much.

I bit the inside of my cheek, trying to focus. My father Óðinn traded his eye for a drink from Mímir's well, and all the knowledge and wisdom flowing through that magical water. I'd always thought he got a bit of a raw deal, but now I reconsidered. If I had Óðinn's wisdom...

I sighed. I had nothing.

"What do you know about horses?" I offered, weakly.

"I'm guessing I know more than you," Hel said. "Hold on." She did not look at me as the chariot jolted forward.

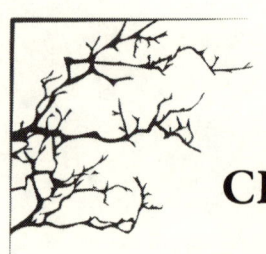

CHAPTER FOUR

"THE THING ABOUT SAILING," I said, raising my voice over the hiss of water against the hull of our little skiff, "is to know how the wind works."

I glanced at Hel. She crouched in the bow, wearing a heavy, dark dress despite the midday heat rippling across the water. She looked uncomfortable, and quite unimpressed.

I carried on anyway. It was our third day together, and I was feeling lucky.

"If the wind comes from the side of the boat, like it is now, it's called—"

"Reaching," Hel said. "And the wind appears to be coming at a right angle to our boat, making this is a beam reach. Correct?"

I muttered something very impolite under my breath. Hel's eyes sparkled in the sunlight.

"You're enjoying this far too much," I said.

The exposed tendons in her neck flexed in the sunlight as Hel turned away from me, showing me the bones on her left side. I was starting to think she turned like that when I actually succeeded in making her smile.

"Well, let's see if I can surprise you, then," I said.

"I doubt it," Hel replied.

I tried not to grin as I leaned on the tiller, turning the little skiff until we were running in the same direction as the wind. It was quieter this direction, with just the purr of the water under our hull. I reached for the mainsheet and let it out, extending the blinding white sail as far as it could go. The waves sliced open before us, sending rainbows of spray across the bow and over our faces.

Damn, what a fantastic day for a sail.

"Oh, yeah!" I shouted. "And now what are we doing, Queen Hel?"

Hel leaned across the bow, her skeletal fingers almost touching the wavetops. She turned to me with a raised eyebrow on her living face, and what looked like a barely suppressed smile on her lips.

"Running," she shouted. "Going downwind is called running."

I smiled at her. Hel was almost standing now, reaching across the bow to the little rainbows flying from the waves. She was off balance. And right behind her was the sort of freakishly large wave I'd been looking for.

"Right," I yelled. "And what about this?"

I shoved the tiller hard, spinning the little boat. We slammed broadside into the big wave. Hel screamed as cold water knocked her off her feet and into my chest. I grabbed her waist instinctively, pulling the tiller back to face the skiff upwind and make sure we wouldn't capsize.

Hel jumped away from me. The boat rocked with her sudden movement. "Oh, you jerk!" she screamed.

I wiped saltwater from my eyes with a grin. "You know what that's called?"

"Being a complete jackass," she said, pushing her wet hair from her eyes.

"I was going to say, 'surprising you.'"

"Well, that was a horrible surprise."

I rolled my eyes. "Oh, don't tell me. You know more about surprising someone too?"

Hel smiled, her eyes dancing. The wave had soaked her heavy dress, making it hug her living side. Her nipple was hard, outlined by the wet fabric. She had a nice breast, I realized. A very nice breast.

Two hands hit me square in the chest. I flew backward out of the boat and crashed into the ocean. The water was cold enough to make me forget all about Hel's perfect breast. I surfaced to the sound of her laughter ringing across the waves.

"Oh, Baldr, I'm sorry, but you should have seen your face!"

"Well, clearly you know more about being a complete jackass than me," I called, swimming back to the boat.

Hel's skeletal hand shot over the side of the boat to splash me. I dunked under the waves, then spat an arc of water toward her. It fell well short of the boat, and she laughed even harder.

There it was again. Her cheek flushed with color, her eyes sparkled, and she actually looked pretty. No, more than just pretty. Despite the bones of her left side, or perhaps because of the contrast, Hel's living side was suddenly gorgeous.

She reached for me as I approached the boat. "Come on. I'll help you."

I took a mouthful of ocean water before I accepted her living hand. She grabbed my wrist and leaned back, helping me scramble into the hull. Once I had the tiller, she pulled away and sat down, smoothing her wet dress across her lap.

"So, Baldr the Beautiful, what's next?" she asked.

I sprayed my mouthful of seawater over her head. She shrieked, pulling up her skirt to cover her face and exposing a considerable amount of leg. Her left thigh was bone and tendons, but it was the creamy, pale skin of her right side that drew me in.

As I tried not to stare, it occurred to me I might actually miss Queen Hel when I returned to Asgard.

BUT, NO MATTER WHAT I tried, I couldn't teach her a damn thing.

Hel knew more than me about chariots, about archery and sword fighting, about farming and sailing. She knew the dozen ways you could make mead, plus a dozen more I'd never heard of. She told me of the Greeks' new science called philosophy, and the Chinese invention of gunpowder. She'd heard of the bloody civil war among the Elves, and she could actually explain the source of the conflict. She even told me how Angrboða had seized power in Jötunheimr. She knew so damned much about everything I started to wonder if she'd had a drink from Mímir's well herself.

It was late afternoon on the third day, the final day, and I was feeling almost desperate. We'd walked along the river after our morning of sailing, and then, after lunch, I asked if we could return to the orchard. This was where Hel seemed the least comfortable; for some reason, this orchard threw her slightly off her game. It was my last, desperate chance. Perhaps I could stumble on something out here.

Or, if I had to beg for more time, this was probably the place to do it.

"Are these all apples?" I asked. I'd given up trying to offer her some knowledge. Instead I was asking a thousand questions in the hopes she'd slip up.

Hel shook her head. Her back was stiff, and she'd turned her living face away from me. The trees around us were flowering, filling the air with their delicious perfume. Soft, white petals drifted in the space between us, falling like snow.

I wished I could ask her why the orchard made her uncomfortable, but I didn't imagine that question would go over particularly well.

"So...pears? Cherries?"

She shook her head again, although I wasn't sure if she was telling me I was wrong or if she was just trying to brush off the stray petals caught in her hair. She was wearing it loose today, and it tumbled down over her shoulders, softening the severe lines of her aggressively unflattering dress.

"Would you even tell me if I guessed?" I asked, with a smile. I picked a blossom from a tree and brought it to my nose. It had a light, sweet fragrance. I examined it. Five soft, white petals unfurled casually from a pollen-laden yellow core.

"Apricots?" I glanced at her.

She looked away so quickly her hair whipped across her shoulders. At the same time her dress snagged on a log hidden in the thick grass, and she stumbled.

I moved without thinking, catching her arm in mine. It was only after I closed my hand around the twin bones of her skeletal forearm that I realized it didn't feel right.

She was warm and soft against my palm. Like skin.

Hel met my eyes and a deep red flush burned across her neck and living cheek. She yanked her arm out of my grasp and stumbled backward.

Interesting. Perhaps she wasn't totally immune to my charms after all.

"Pardon me," I said, holding my hands up in front of me. "I just didn't want you to break your nose."

Her lips twitched with the barest hint of a smile, and an absolutely insane idea bubbled through my consciousness.

"Oh, there is something I can teach you," I whispered.

"Excuse me?"

I stepped closer to her, so close our chests almost touched. Her back stiffened, although she held her ground. I met her eyes, trying not to be distracted by the way her breath was suddenly coming faster.

"You'd have to trust me," I said.

She laughed. It sounded forced. "Trust you? You really think you could do anything to hurt me?"

"I'd never hurt you," I said.

I raised my hand and ran my fingers softly along the curve of her living cheek. Her entire body shivered in response, but she didn't back away.

"And we should be somewhere private. Where we won't be interrupted."

"I know all about sex," she hissed. But her voice trembled.

"I'm sure you do." I dropped my fingers, tracing the line of her jaw. "You've read all the books."

She inhaled sharply as I ran my thumb down her neck. Her pulse raced under my touch.

"Stop," she whispered.

I dropped my hand and met her eyes. A storm of emotions rolled through their pale blue depths, and tears pooled in the corner of both her living and her empty, skeletal eye. Some distant part of my mind realized I didn't mind looking at her anymore.

No, more than that.

I wanted her.

"Hel," I said, surprised by the roughness in my voice. "There is something I'm very good at, and I'd like to show you. But you have to want it too."

Her living cheek turned bright red. She pulled her bottom lip into her mouth and bit it. That shouldn't have turned me on - nothing about her should turn me on - but my body responded just the same. I'd been intimate with so many women, and more than a few men, because they were pretty or useful. It was a nice change to want someone because she was interesting.

"If I say no," she whispered. "What happens?"

I held my hands up. "I walk away. You win. This is the only thing I have left, Hel."

She closed her living eye. A tear pushed through her eyelashes and ran down her pale cheek, trembling on her jawline. I wanted to wipe it away, but I forced myself to stand still. A single flower petal fell on her collarbone, winking in the golden sunlight.

"The orchard is private," she said, without opening her eyes.

I blinked in surprise. "Here?"

"No one comes here. Not unless I ask."

I held my breath. Oh, by the Realms, I wanted to crush her to my chest. I wanted to taste her, to know if the rest of her would feel warm and soft too.

She wiped her cheek with the back of her hand and took a deep breath. "Yes," she whispered. "But don't...don't tell anyone."

I grinned. "My Lady, you have my word."

Her pale eye opened and met mine. She looked smaller, somehow, as though she were suddenly vulnerable.

"What do I do?" she asked.

I pulled her into my arms and kissed her.

I wasn't sure what to expect, if it would feel soft like grabbing her arm or if I'd feel the hard scrape of bone against my mouth, but I couldn't resist any longer. She looked so innocent, and so scared. I wanted to comfort her.

I wanted to taste her.

Her lips felt soft and full against mine. I moved across them gently, feeling the hiss of air as she inhaled. I smiled before kissing her again, more urgently, tilting my head to meet her. I wrapped my arm around her waist, running my hand over the rough cloth of her ridiculously ugly dress as I pressed my mouth against hers, asking for more.

She pulled back, shaking her head. "I don't know how to kiss," she said, her voice shaky and her breath uneven.

"You're doing just fine." I already missed her soft weight in my arms.

She took a deep breath and smoothed the front of her dress. Her shoulders trembled. "I should lie down," she said, looking at the petal-strewn grass beneath her feet.

Something golden flashed in the space between us. I froze. Hel panted as she stared intently at the ground. And with each ragged exhale, something flickered across her skin, like a slow ripple of light over water. When I wrapped my fingers gently around her wrist, the pulse of light flashed again, stronger and brighter.

"Do you want to lie down?" I asked.

She shook her head. "Yes. I mean, I don't know. I don't..."

I stepped closer, turning my waist so I didn't impale her with my hard-on, and leaned into her neck, running my lips softly along her skin as I reached around her back for the seam of that horrible dress. I kissed her lightly, listening to her breath catch in her throat as I unbuckled the row of clasps along her back. Her pulse raced, and golden sparks sizzled across her skin as I touched her. I wondered if she noticed them.

When the last clasp was undone, I raised my hand to her shoulder and gently slid the dress down her arms and over her waist. Then I stepped back, smiling at her.

She had a surprisingly lovely body, curvy and soft. Her breast was every bit as perfect as I'd imagined. Even her skeletal side seemed vulnerable, not terrifying. I realized I might be the first person to actually see Hel naked. The ripples of light flashed faster and brighter now, obscuring her body as they washed over her. No, maybe not obscuring. It was almost as if there was something else underneath.

Hel hesitated, her brow furrowing. The ripples of light stopped moving over her body and I realized she was holding her breath. She looked like she was about to cry.

"You okay?" I asked, wrapping my hand around her waist.

"You're looking at me," she whispered.

I kissed her again. This time she opened for me, leaning into me, allowing me to explore her secret, hidden places with my tongue. I fell into our kiss, pulling her chest to mine, feeling her breast swell against me as her chest rose with her frantic, panting breaths.

"I like looking at you," I said, when we pulled apart. "You're fascinating."

She trembled, hiding her face against my neck, and I realized the truth of my words. Hel was fascinating; she was the single most fascinating woman I'd ever met.

"Let's lie down," I said.

Hel nodded and pulled back, stepping out of her dress. She didn't meet my eyes as she lay down on the petal-strewn grass. Her naked body flashed and rippled with light. I didn't dare ask about it.

"Will it hurt?" she asked, her eyes wide. "I've read that it hurts, the first time."

I lay down next to her living side, weaving my fingers with hers. "I'm not going to hurt you."

I brought her hand to my lips and kissed every finger, moving slowly, watching her chest rise and fall. Sometimes, as the web of light surrounding her rippled and crackled, I could see two breasts, their twin nipples tight as rosebuds.

I turned her hand over and brought my lips to her wrist, feeling her pulse race against my mouth. My lips moved slowly up her arm, kissing her as the golden light surged around me. She was gasping by the time I reached her chest, and she cried out when I closed my lips over her nipple. Her scent overwhelmed me, and I struggled with the dull throb in my groin. Oh, damn, I wanted her.

I closed my teeth gently around the hard bud of her nipple, and her back arched beneath me. My hand slid down, leaving the soft curve of her chest and caressing her stomach. Her breath stuttered as my hand reached her thighs. I gave Hel's perfect breast one final kiss and watched her face as my fingers moved between her legs.

Her eyes closed. Both eyes, although I hadn't been certain her skeletal half had an eyelid. The golden light poured over her now, pulsing in rhythm with her breathing, and her lips parted.

I caressed the curls outside her sex, waiting and watching for her reaction. Hel groaned, moving her hips into my hand, and I slipped a finger into her folds. She was slick and wet; heat poured from her, bathing my palm. My hand circled her lips, pressing gently as she panted under me, searching for the tight little bud at the apex of her sex.

She gasped when I found it, and her legs tensed around my hand. For a moment I thought that was enough, that I'd brought her to climax with one touch. But she lifted her hips again, moaning a single word.

"More."

I grinned. The sweet tang of her sex filled the orchard, and I had to stop myself from grinding my hips into the ground, searching for my own release. Light burst from her body, flooding the orchard, spilling onto the grass, and transforming the white petals into flecks of gold. I tried to look through the light, like I'd looked through the gleam of sunlight on the water water to judge distance to the ocean bottom. It was insanely hard to focus; she panted and rippled beneath me, and every instinct in my body cried out to fill her, to take her, to satisfy her.

Then I saw, and my heart stopped.

At the same moment she cried out, her entire body stiffening beneath me. Light exploded the space between us, and she lay beneath it, naked and glorious on a bed of flower petals. Her eyes were closed, her rosebud lips parted, her full breasts heaving as she tried to catch her breath.

I had never seen a more beautiful woman.

My entire life I'd lived in Asgard, among the Æsir, who are more beautiful than mortal women. And Freyja is the most beautiful Æsir, with her golden hair, ruby lips, and generous breasts. But the woman trembling beneath my hands was more beautiful than Freyja. Her red-gold hair alone was more spectacular than Freyja's, or Sif's, or...

Hel's pale blue eyes opened. Those, at least, I recognized. Her soft lips curved into a smile. My heart broke. I was lost, and I knew it. I'd do anything for that smile.

"Baldr," she gasped. "What was—"

My face must have given me away. Hel frowned and pulled herself up, staring down at her body.

She screamed.

The pain in her voice twisted my heart, and I reached for her. She flinched, pulling away from my arm.

"Get out of here!" she yelled.

"Wait!" I grabbed her ankle, closing my hands around her pale skin.

A second later white spots exploded across my vision as my head rocked back. The sharp metallic tang of blood filled the back of my mouth. I spat, slowly realizing she'd kicked me. In the face.

"What just happened?" I said.

Hel backed up against a tree trunk, her legs pulled to her chest. Tears streamed down her round cheeks.

"Please, let me help," I said.

She shook her head and vanished, leaving white petals swirling in her wake.

"Hel!" I screamed.

I wiped my mouth with the back of my hand, and it came away bloody. I called her name again, over and over, begging her to come back, long after I realized it wasn't going to happen.

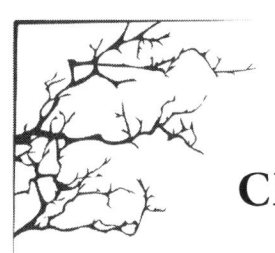

CHAPTER FIVE

HEL'S ORCHARD WAS ENORMOUS, and I got lost almost instantaneously. It didn't help that my mind was swirling, and I couldn't remember a thing about our walk out here, aside from the way Hel hid her face by turning to the side. Or the flower petals that stuck to her dark hair. And to her arms and legs as she lay on the ground, naked before me.

I groaned. It was half tempting to think Hel's transformation was a dream. But when I brought my fingers to my face, I could smell the sweet tang of her glorious sex.

Not a dream, then.

The sky faded from periwinkle to sapphire to an ominous midnight blue before the light vanished entirely. I was still wandering in the dark, wondering if I was about to walk off a cliff and break whatever could still be broken when you're dead.

After what felt like an entire lifetime, I saw the distant, orange flicker of torches. I followed the lights and found myself back at the castle. No one seemed to much care if I came or went, so I wandered into the feast hall. Someone offered me a flagon of mead, but I shook my head. If I started drinking right now, I might never stop.

The door to the narrow hallway was closed. I pushed it open anyway. The hall was dark and silent. I walked slowly, listening to the desolate echo of my footsteps, until I came to the room where I first met Hel.

No one was there.

My shoulders trembled. The torch in my hands shivered, its flame casting wild, desperate shadows along the walls. Of course she wouldn't be here.

"Baldr?" a quiet voice asked softly from behind me.

I pulled myself together and turned. "That's me."

It was Eriksen, watching me with a very strange expression. "Are you looking for something, my Lord?"

It was all I could do not to laugh. *Oh, me? I'm just looking for the most beautiful woman in the Nine Realms. You know, the one who's half dead with maggots in her chest?*

"No, nothing. I just seem to have forgotten how to get to my quarters."

I could tell from the thin press of his lips that Eriksen didn't buy a word of it. "If you'll please follow me," he said.

I did as I was told.

A SHARP KNOCK ON MY door jolted me out of my daze just after sunrise. I pressed my palms against my eyes before pulling myself out of the chair. I hadn't been sleeping, exactly, but I didn't feel entirely awake either. I'd spent the whole night hunched in that armchair, or pacing the room, trying to untangle the complicated mess of obligations and longing my afterlife had become.

"Come in," I called.

The door opened. A thin, severe looking woman I didn't recognize stood in the hallway. "Hel requests your presence," she said.

"Really?" My heart leapt. "Now?"

The woman sniffed, looking me over with a frown. "As soon as you're presentable."

I glanced down at my wrinkled clothes. There were grass stains on my knees from the orchard, and I'd shoved my sleeves up about a thousand times last night as I paced the floor.

"Right." I tried to give her a charming smile. "And where would I find a suitable outfit?"

"I suggest the wardrobe," she said, pulling the door closed behind her.

I opened the enormous wardrobe and groaned. It was packed with supremely uncomfortable clothes. I finally settled on heavy golden robes, stiff black pants, and a white tunic that had been bleached until it felt like wood against my skin. I tried to open the laces at the top of the tunic, in the desperate hopes a hint of chest might help me make whatever case I was going to make, but I couldn't get the shirt to cooperate. In the end I just ran my fingers through my hair and decided to hope for the best.

The woman stood outside my door, pointedly tapping her toe. "Ready, then?" she asked, making it sound as if she'd been waiting for days.

"Of course," I said, with a forced smile.

We walked for a long time, passing rooms I didn't recognize at all. Apparently this palace had a ballroom. And what looked like an indoor garden. My heart sank the further we walked. I'd only spent three days with Hel. I knew nothing of her palace, and next to nothing about her.

My guide cleared her throat. "Through those doors," she announced.

I swallowed. Before me were the biggest set of doors I'd ever seen. They were ebony, and set with dark, sparkling gems which gleamed in the flickering torchlight. I took a deep breath and stepped forward.

The doors swung open as I approached, revealing a cavernous throne room. It wasn't exactly crowded, but there were more people inside than I'd ever seen in the palace. And they were all watching me. I tried to smile as I raised my eyes to the dais at the end of the room.

Hel sat on her throne. It was huge, and black, and it looked supremely uncomfortable. Her robes cascaded off her shoulders, rolling down the steps of the dais behind her. At least the robes on her human half did; her skeletal half was draped in dark, rotting tatters, as usual. The flickering orange torchlight played off her exposed bones, making her look especially formidable.

Ah. Just in case I thought we were getting close, then.

I walked slowly, keeping my eyes on Hel. Her face was a blank mask, betraying nothing. When I was about five steps from her throne, she raised her left hand, flashing bones and decaying tendons. I stopped and swallowed. Hard.

"Eriksen. Please read the terms of my agreement with Baldr, son of Óðinn," Hel said. Her cold voice reverberated through the room.

Eriksen stepped forward and cleared his throat as he unrolled an enormous scroll. He looked especially pale, and I wondered how often Hel actually used this room.

"Thus agreed," he began, "between Baldr Óðinnsen, late of the realm of Asgard, and Hel Lokisdóttir, ruler of the realm of Niflhel. Baldr, son of Óðinn, commits to providing the Lady Hel with some manner of information previously unknown to the Lady, in exchange for which he shall be granted a boon." Eriksen shifted uncomfortably on his feet.

"Thank you," said Hel. She turned her ice-blue eyes to me without the slightest flicker of emotion. "Baldr, son of Óðinn, you have fulfilled your task."

There was a slight gasp from the crowd. I ignored it

"I shall now return you to Asgard," Hel said. She raised her left hand again, and a cold wind billowed from behind the throne, lifting my hair and pressing the stiff fabric of my shirt against my chest.

"No," I said. I had to raise my voice to be heard above the hiss of the wind.

Hel's hand trembled and the wind vanished. "Excuse me?"

"Eriksen, could you read that again?" I asked.

Eriksen raised both eyebrows, looking so uncomfortable it almost hurt to watch. He glanced at Hel. She gave him the barest nod. He picked up the parchment again, holding it like a shield before his chest.

"Thus agreed," he began.

"Just summarize it for me. Please."

The tall, thin man wavered, and for a minute I worried he was about to pass out. Then he coughed slightly and straightened the parchment. "The agreement states Baldr will provide Hel with new information, in exchange for a boon."

The hall fell silent. Hel raised an eyebrow at me.

"Thank you," I said, grateful my voice managed to carry a measure of confidence I didn't exactly feel. "The agreement said a boon. Not a return to Asgard."

The corner of Hel's mouth twitched. "What are you saying?"

I took a deep breath. "My Lady Hel. I wish to be your consort."

Someone in the crowd dropped something metallic, and the crash reverberated through the entire throne room. Hel's eyes flashed.

"You mock me before my own subjects?" she demanded.

I spread my arms wide and dropped to one knee. "I do not."

The slightest flicker of light danced across Hel's shoulders and rippled down her body. "You're out of your mind, Óðinnsen."

"My Lady. You are the most fascinating woman in the Nine Realms. I wish to be with you. That is my boon. Send me from your castle, if you must, but I will not return to Asgard. As long as you are here, I'll remain in Niflhel."

There was a scattered murmur behind me. Hel's lips parted for an instant, then clamped shut.

"And what of your duties, Baldr the Beautiful? The role you play among the Æsir?"

I shook my head. This was what kept me up all night, and there was nothing to do now but tell the truth. "My Lady, I've spent a lifetime serving the Æsir. I mend conflicts, I let each side vent their frustrations to me instead of each other. I've done Óðinn's bidding, going wherever he thought a pretty face would help him advance his agenda."

I paused, reaching for the words. "It's not a role I chose, my Lady. Now that death has freed me of those obligations, I find I'm reluctant to return."

Hel shifted on her throne, showing me only the naked bones of her left side. "And your wife? Nanna Nepsdóttir?"

"I suppose I loved her," I said. "I tried to be a good husband, at least. But now, if I returned to Asgard, I would have to tell her I desire another."

That did it. The crowd behind me all started talking at once, and another ripple of light flashed across Hel's body.

"Stop!" Hel rose to her feet, and the voices died in an instant. "Leave us. All of you."

She stood, impassive and foreboding, as the room emptied. I got a few sympathetic glances from the crowd, although most of them gawked at me openly. I tried to smile, to look relaxed and confident, although I felt none of those things.

Finally the massive doors slammed behind us, and we were alone in the vast, echoing room. Hel looked down at me from her imposing throne.

"What the fuck are you playing at?" she said, shoving her massive skirts behind her as she descended the steps.

She looked majestic in her dark robes, with her eyes burning against her pale skin. My cock twitched inside the stiff, heavy pants and I bit my tongue, just enough to tamp down my arousal. I really shouldn't have been turned on at this point, but after yesterday, I couldn't help it.

"In all my long years ruling Niflhel, I've never agreed to send anyone back. Why would you defy me?" She reached the end of the dais and jumped down, sweeping across the polished floor. "You have nothing to gain from this, Baldr."

I came to my feet as she approached. She stopped several paces from me, pulling herself up and crossing her arms over her chest. Her black hair fluttered over her bare neck.

"I demand an explanation!"

I smiled at her and spread my arms wide. "I'd like to be your consort."

"Damn you!" she spat. "Did you just want to humiliate me? Did you want everyone to know you've turned me into a...a harlot?"

I took a step closer, closing the distance between us. Her back stiffened.

"Are you trying to...to..." she stammered.

I bent to her left side, her dead side, and kissed her cheek. It looked like raw bones, but it felt soft and warm under my lips. I closed my eyes, trusting touch and taste to reveal the beauty I could not see. She smelled good, sweet and delicate, like the gentle perfume of the flowers in the orchard. I kissed her neck, enjoying the flutter of her pulse.

"Baldr. Why are you doing this?"

I brought my hand to the curve of her hip. "I want to," I whispered. "I like kissing you."

"No. Stop it." She pulled away and stepped backward. "Damn it, look at me." Her voice trembled and she turned away. The white of her skull flashed in the torchlight.

I grinned. "I hate to break it to you, Lady Hel, but I actually already know what you look like. Better than most, I'm guessing."

Her collarbone trembled. I reached for her hand, closing my fingers around her wrist. When she didn't pull away, I brought it to my lips, kissing the delicate, invisible skin on the inside of her wrist.

"You don't feel dead," I said. "Is it a curse, then?"

Light shivered across her body, and she pulled away from my arms. "What does it matter?" she hissed, her eyes flashing.

"I'm sorry," I stammered. "I didn't mean—"

"You want to save me, is that it? To break the curse and drag me back to Asgard, your pretty little prize from the time you went to Niflhel?"

She took another step backward. The air between us crackled with golden light.

"I don't need your help! Niflhel is mine, Óðinnsen. I'm never returning to the living realms!"

"That's not what I meant!" I snapped. "Listen to me. I don't want to take you anywhere. Shit, I don't want to go back to Asgard myself! That's what I'm trying to tell you!"

Her lip quivered. I stepped forward and grabbed her wrist.

"I swear to you, Hel, what you look like doesn't matter to me. Cursed or not, I just want the chance to be with you. Right here, in your realm."

She made a strange, strangled sound. It took me a minute to realize Hel Lokisdóttir, Queen of the Realm of Inglorious Dead, was trying not to cry. She hid her face against my chest, and her body shook in my arms. I held her for a long time as light surged across her back and arms, flowing over both of us. When I finally noticed her hair had changed from stringy black to the full red-gold waves I'd seen in the orchard, I wasn't even sure when it had happened.

Hel sniffed against my chest, then pulled away. Her eyes were rimmed with red, and her teeth bit at her lower lip. Even so, my breath caught in my throat. She was easily the most beautiful woman I'd ever seen. Men would die for her, I realized. She could send whole troops to their death, and they would go. Gladly.

"Is this what you wanted?" she asked. Her eyes flashed defiance, even as her shoulders trembled.

I swallowed. "You... Hel, you're so beautiful."

Her shoulders hitched. "I know."

By the Nine Realms, she looked miserable. I ran my fingers over the soft curve of her cheek.

"Do you know how rare it is for anyone to surprise me?" I asked. "And yet you've done it, over and over again. You fascinate me, Hel. That's why I want to stay here, and that's why I want to be your consort. If you'll have me."

Her eyes flickered over me, wide and blue.

"And what I just said still holds. I really don't care what you look like, my lady."

Her lips curved into the barest hint of a smile. "The first person I allow to return, and you refuse me. You're an idiot, Baldr."

"You'd be surprised how often I hear that."

Her smiled widened by a tiny fraction. She sighed and glanced away, showing me the left side of her face.

"It's not a curse," she whispered. "It's a spell. It's my spell."

"Your spell?"

My mind spun. Of course, almost all of the Æsir can cast spells. I have half a dozen runes I employ in battle, and most of us can travel through the aether. But to cast a spell that obscures your entire body, all the time...Damn. There was only one other person in the Nine Realms who had powers like that; her father, Loki the Lie-smith.

Hel blinked furiously, avoiding eye contact. I took a deep breath and tried to pick my words carefully.

"That's amazing, Hel. I had no idea anyone could do something like that. Isn't it exhausting?"

She didn't meet my gaze, but I saw her smile. "It does require a certain level of concentration."

"So are you saying I broke your concentration yesterday?"

Her neck and cheeks flushed a delicate pink. "Uh," she stammered, "I just didn't know what to expect..."

I leaned close to her, running my lips along her neck, breathing in her sweet, floral scent. "My lady, I would be delighted to break your concentration again."

She whimpered. Oh, that did it. The urge to hold her, to taste her, to feel every part of her body against mine flooded through me. I moved my hips against hers, letting her feel the hard length of my cock for the first time. She gasped, and I covered her mouth with mine, pressing against her soft, full lips, filling her. She opened for me, returning my kiss with furiosity. My blood surged, pounding in my ears, and I ran my hand along the back of her dress, searching for the seams.

She pulled away. "Not here," she gasped. "Please. Give me a minute."

I stifled a groan. It was impossible to look at her and not want to kiss her, to run my fingers through the red-gold of her hair or press my chest against the soft curves of hers.

She took a few deep breaths and turned away. Her back stiffened and she moaned as her body shuddered and blazed with light. When she turned back to me, she was wearing the illusion; her right side was pale, and her left side dead.

"Does it hurt?" I asked.

The right side of her face twisted into a wry grin. "Of course."

I reached for her hand, but she pulled away. "No. Please, don't touch me. I'm having a hard enough time concentrating as it is."

She smiled and a shiver of light ran down her body. My cock stiffened, throbbing against the seam of my pants. Damn, this woman did it for me, no matter what form she wore. I ignored the surprisingly strong impulse to grab her and fuck her against the steps to her own throne.

"Follow me," she said.

I followed, wishing the dress she wore was tighter.

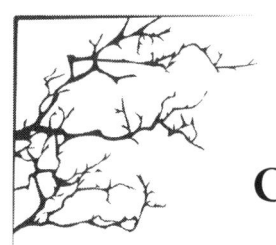

CHAPTER SIX

ERIKSEN WAITED FOR her outside the door to the throne room. He frowned at me, but bowed low before Hel.

"Eriksen," Hel said. "I'm going to retire to my chambers. Please let the advisors know I'll reschedule our meeting."

"Of course," Eriksen murmured. He raised an eyebrow at me. "And the Æsir?"

Hel cleared her throat and straightened her back. "Baldr will be accompanying me."

Eriksen's face turned several shades whiter. "My Queen?"

"No, I have not been enchanted," she said, a delicate blush spreading over the pale cheek of her living side. "And I've not lost my mind. And could you please tell everyone I'm going to expect a full update tomorrow?"

Eriksen was gasping like a tall, pale fish. "Of course. Yes. Of course, my Queen."

Hel turned back to me, her cheek and neck flushed crimson. It was so damn cute I had to lean forward and kiss her.

"Stop it," she whispered, giving me a coy smile with the living side of her face.

I almost kissed her again, but I saw Eriksen rocking on his feet. His face had gone from pale to a sickly sort of light green, and I figured he'd probably been pushed far enough out of his comfort zone for one morning.

Well, almost far enough.

I winked at him as we left.

AFTER A FEW TWISTS and turns, we stopped at a set of wooden doors. Hel raised her hand, and the doors opened. I followed her into a small, circular room with a recessed window, a desk, several bookcases, and a narrow bed. The doors shut behind us, and I noticed they were barred from the inside.

"What's this?" I asked, running my fingers along the heavy bar next to the door.

Hel turned away. "It's for the nights. I can't hold my illusion while I sleep. I need to make sure I'm never discovered."

"Wait." I blinked, examining the sparse room a second time. I'd assumed Hel had taken me to the closest private place, maybe a room for visiting servants. "These are your chambers?"

"Of course."

"Well, you've done it again," I said. "I'm surprised."

Hel shrugged. "Why would I need more than this?"

"I can think of a few reasons for getting a bigger bed."

"I didn't furnish my chambers with you in mind, Baldr." Her voice was sharp, but the hint of a smile played across the corner of her mouth.

I shrugged off my heavy cape and pulled the stiff, uncomfortable shirt over my head. Hel's eyes widened as I folded the shirt and lay it gently on the table. Golden sparks danced down her arms as she inhaled sharply.

"Am I ruining your concentration, my Lady?"

Golden light filled the room, obscuring her body. When the sparks faded, I was once again facing the most beautiful woman in the Nine Realms. And her arms were bent, unbuttoning the back of her heavy, black dress.

Hel gave me a shy, hesitant smile as she slid the dress down her arms, exposing her glorious breasts. I moaned as she stepped out of her clothes. If I hadn't already been dead, the sight of her naked would have killed me.

"Oh, have mercy," I whispered, stepping toward her. I couldn't resist; the pull of her naked body was stronger than gravity.

She frowned. "Baldr, I'm such a hypocrite," she whispered, turning to show me the left side of her face.

I reached for her cheek, surprised to find my hands trembling. "What is it?"

"I've spent my whole life hiding this form. And now, it pleases me to see you enjoy it."

I opened my mouth to tell her something, anything, but she raised her hand to my naked chest, and all I could do was gasp. Her blue eyes watched me as her hand explored my chest, dropping to the waist of my pants. I shuddered as her fingers whispered across the hot throb of my erection.

"May I?" she asked.

"Please," I moaned.

Hel frowned in concentration, trying to untie the stupidly complex knots of my waistband. I helped her, gently sliding my pants down my hips. I felt absurdly aware of my own nakedness, and my stiff cock pressing against the soft curve of her stomach. Her soft fingers slid over my length, caressing me gently, hesitantly. It wasn't until I gasped at her touch that I realized I'd been holding my breath.

"It's too big," she said.

I tried to respond, but with her hand wrapped around the head of my cock, I couldn't exactly form words.

"There's no way that could fit inside me," she whispered.

Her grip tightened and my whole body shuddered, curving around her.

Hel froze, her eyes cloudy. "Are you—"

"F-feels good," I stammered. "You. Feel good."

Her eyes lit up and her hand moved, flickering gently up to the head. "I do?"

I moaned into her neck. Her touch flooded my body with heat, concentrating all my attention. Hel's skin was smooth against mine, and her smell filled the air between us. I wanted to grab her, to push her to the floor and fill her, over and over, but I forced myself to hold still as she explored my body.

She stroked me slowly, tentatively, until my entire body was rigid and shaking, gasping with pleasure. I trembled on the edge of release; she'd brought me so close, so quickly, with just the brush of her hand, the press of her soft curves, and the thick scent of her arousal.

"Hel," I whispered, "if you don't stop, I'm going to—"

She turned and kissed my neck, her lips and tongue flickering across my skin, sending bolts of pleasure through my body.

"I don't want to stop," she said.

My head rocked back, and I let myself go. Her touch filled every part of me, igniting me. I gasped her name as I shuddered in her hands, my climax coating the soft skin of her stomach.

She giggled. It was such a joyful, innocent sound, and it took me a second to realize it had come from Hel. I blinked, my mind staggering back to reality.

"I can please you," she said. She sounded out of breath.

I grinned. "Oh, yes. You do please me."

Her blue eyes met mine, and her lips parted. I kissed her before she could say anything, kissed her deep and hard, for a long time, giving vent to all the passion I held back while I let her explore my body. I ran my hands over her hips as my tongue entered her, letting my fingers follow the gentle curve of her belly, pausing at the curls of hair surrounding her sex.

Hel moaned into my mouth, and I dropped my hand, pressing my finger into her folds. She was slick and wet, her little bud a hard, swollen nub. Her back stiffened as I rubbed it, and my cock surged in response, twitching against her thigh.

I broke off our kiss, leaving her gasping. "Lie down," I said. "Please. There's so much more I'd like to show you."

She nodded and stumbled backward, landing heavily on her narrow bed. Her eyes widened as I lowered myself over her, and I realized she expected me to fuck her right there. Oh, damn, but it was tempting.

I bit the inside of my lip to damp down my own arousal and started kissing her, softly, along her neck and collarbone. She moaned when I turned to her perfect breasts, cupping one in my hand and running my tongue along the swell of the other. I traced the tight rosebud of her nipple with my lips, then wrapped my teeth around it and pressed until she cried out, her back arching under me.

"Baldr," she sighed. "It feels good. You feel so good."

I hummed in response, sliding my hand along the curve of her stomach and through the curls between her legs. I pressed into the heat of her sex, brushing her clit with my fingers as I licked and sucked her nipple. Her hips started to move, rocking against my hand.

She was close. Oh, damn, she was close.

I wanted to make her come right then, but I backed off, sliding my hand down her thigh and giving her nipple a final, gentle kiss.

"W-what's wrong?" she whimpered.

"Nothing is wrong," I said. "I just want to taste you."

Her eyes widened. "Taste...me?"

I watched her as I dropped my head between her legs. Understanding lit her face a moment before her eyes rolled back in pleasure.

Oh, her taste! Dipping my tongue into her wet folds was bliss. My cock throbbed in response, making me want to thrust my hips against her mattress, seeking another release. Her fingers plunged into my hair, twisting against my skin, and I moaned in pleasure. Her hips crashed into my lips, and she cried as she writhed under me, calling my name over and over until it sounded like supplication, or prayer.

I tried to keep her there as long as possible, hovering over her clit, then devouring her with my tongue and lips, backing off whenever her body began to stiffen under mine. When she finally came, it was so intense I almost came along with her. She arched her back, screaming my name as her thighs clamped around my head. I closed my eyes and soaked up her heat, savoring her bliss.

When her legs fell back to the bed, I lowered myself onto the hard mattress next to her. Her fiery golden hair lay matted against her sweaty cheeks and forehead. I brushed it back, and she turned to smile at me.

"I had no idea," she gasped.

Another jolt of arousal ran through me like fire. I took a deep breath, trying to read her. Some women want more after an orgasm like that, and some want to sleep. If she was the latter, I told myself, I'd just have to take care of things myself as soon as she was asleep. My cock throbbed painfully, and I tried to ignore it.

I kissed her cheek, then the curve of her jaw. She moaned, shifting to press her body against mine. Oh, damn. I shivered as my cock pulsed, urging me to get closer to this beautiful woman. I trailed my fingers up the inside of her thigh, watching her eyes widen as her lips parted.

"Do you still feel good?" I asked.

"Oh!" she cried, her perfect lips curving into a smile. "I feel so strange. Like being pulled apart and then put back together."

"Is that good?" My hand reached the dark curls between her legs. I brushed them very gently.

"Yes," she sighed, her hips tilting to meet my touch. "But, I think I want more."

My cock ached and arousal throbbed through me, insistently, as irresistible as the tide. I rolled over, holding my body above hers. Very gently, I pressed the head of my cock to the apex of her sex, rubbing her nub.

"Do you want to see if I fit?" I said.

Her eyes widened and her hips rolled against mine. Heat poured off her, making it very hard to remain still.

"We don't have to," I managed to stammer. "I can just...keep doing this." My hips rubbed against hers, rewarded with another flush of heat from her body.

"This feels good," she said. "But, I don't think it's enough."

I grinned at her wide eyes, her flushed cheeks. "I can give you more."

She moaned and rocked against me. "It's like an ache, somewhere deep inside. Yes. Yes, I want more."

"Oh, my Lady," I growled as I pressed my lips to hers, lowering myself onto her body.

It took everything I had to enter her slowly. I kept one hand on her clit, rubbing her gently as I pressed inside her. Still, I almost lost it once she rippled under me, her glorious body rocking against mine, her sweet heat embracing me.

She yelped, and I pulled back immediately. Her hands wrapped around my legs, pressing me closer.

"No, don't stop," she moaned. "It hurt for a second, but, oh, it doesn't hurt any more."

I held my breath and pressed into her, entering her fully. She gasped, arching her back as her legs tightened around my thighs. The sight of her body spread before me, lips parted, eyes rolled back, almost undid me. When was the last time I'd wanted so desperately to please a woman?

I closed my teeth around my tongue, trying to focus as I caressed her hard nub, watching her body react. Only when she began rocking her hips against mine did I move inside her, thrusting as slowly as I could, following her lead. Oh, she was so tight around my cock, and so hot. I could feel every shiver, every way her body responded to my touch.

"What magic is this?" she gasped as her entire body began to tremble.

I pushed harder, thrusting into her as I rubbed my fingers against her clit. She gasped, her hands digging into my shoulders, twining through my hair. As she came, her pleasure surged through me, her heat and release entering me, spurring me on. Her body tightened around me, and she felt so good I could no longer hold back.

I wrapped my hands around her hips and crashed into her, finally giving in to the impulse to fill her, to lose myself in her. I exploded inside of her, coming hard for longer than I would have thought possible, oblivious to everything but the pleasure she brought me.

When my vision finally returned to normal, Hel was smiling beneath me, the light through her window washing her exquisite features in delicate cerulean. She looked so beautiful, almost delicate, and a shiver of apprehension danced down my spine.

"Are you okay?" I asked. "I'm sorry, I didn't mean to be so rough."

Her smiled widened, dreamy and blissful. "So that's what it's like. I can see why it drives the mortals mad."

I shifted to her side, not wanting to crush her. I couldn't help a sigh as I eased out of her warm body. "Well, it drives the Æsir mad, too. You should see the way men lose their minds around Freyja. Even Óðinn."

Hel ran her fingers along my cheek. "Thank you," she whispered.

Damn, I just finished fucking her, and already shivers of arousal rippled from her touch. My cock twitched against the smooth curve of her thigh, and her eyes widened.

"Can we do it again?" she asked.

I grinned. Now how was I supposed to refuse that?

CHAPTER SEVEN

HEL'S NARROW SINGLE bed was beyond uncomfortable. After making love for the fifth time - or had it been the sixth? - we'd both collapsed in exhaustion. But I'd woken shortly afterward, crushed against the cold stone wall and unwilling to move Hel's gorgeous sleeping body. I tried sleeping on the floor, which was even worse than the bed, not to mention freezing. I finally ended up in the chair at her desk, dozing in little fits and starts.

Now I stood at her window, watching dawn begin in Niflhel. Hel's window had an amazing view. It must have been built, I realized, so no one could look in on her while she slept. There were no other buildings in sight, not so much as a window ledge. Just a lovely, uninterrupted view of the river, the rolling foothills, and the jagged black mountains. The sky turned a pale turquoise as I watched, improving the view with each passing minute.

But I wasn't overly interested in the scenery. I was watching Hel sleep.

She lay on her side, with her face to the wall. The blanket had fallen off her shoulder, and one elegant long leg poked out, her toes pointed at the window like a dancer. My body hummed in response as the light grew, caressing her soft skin. I would've thought last night used me up, but my cock stiffened as my eyes traced the curve of that leg, from her ankle to the swell of her calf to the thin strip of thigh peeking out from under the dark covers.

I wrapped my hand around my cock and stroked once, remembering the feel of Hel's fingers last night. And the other parts of her body. She sighed in her sleep and more of the blanket slipped from her shoulder, revealing the smooth skin of her back. My hand tightened and my breath caught in my throat.

Damn, this woman was amazing. When was the last time I'd been this turned on? I closed my eyes, leaning against the cold wall as I ran my hand gently over the stiff length of my cock.

I'd lost my head over a few women, back when I first discovered the pleasures of sex. They were mortal, of course; I always watched myself too closely with the Æsir to really fall in love. Kirstin I remembered, the mortal woman who lived at the edge of the forest, the one with raven hair and lips like strawberries. She'd done this to me, filled me with a hunger that seemed like it would never be satiated. Until the day Óðinn called me to his throne to show me what happened to Loki's mortal lovers. I told myself he wasn't threatening me, but still, the vision scared me. I never saw Kristin again.

When I first married Nanna, I'd hoped our marriage vows might create the same sense of excitement and urgency I'd so briefly enjoyed with my first lovers, despite the fact that our matrimony was a contract drawn up by our parents without any input from either of us. Perhaps, in retrospect, I was a fool for hoping passion would grow in such cold, formal ground.

But if those first few days of married life had been with Hel... My cock stiffened against my palm, and I bit back a groan. Last night was amazing. It was everything I'd once hoped I'd find with a wife.

The covers rustled as Hel shifted, and my eyes flew open. I dropped my hands and slammed down on the chair, leaning forward so Hel's desk would cover my raging erection. I'd learned a fair amount about women over my long lifetime, and I was willing to guess Hel would be freaked out by me jacking off while she slept. Or telling her I was fantasizing about marriage after one night together.

Hel yawned and blinked, a slow smile spreading over her face when she saw me. "Baldr. I thought you may have been a dream."

My heart clenched. "No, gorgeous. I'm real."

Her delicate features frowned as she sat up, regrettably pulling the blanket over her breasts. "Yet you look so serious. Is something bothering you?"

How could she tell, damn it? I'd only known this woman a handful of days, and already she could read me. I ran my hand through my hair, searching for something to say. And of course, there was something on my mind, a question that had been driving me crazy all night.

"You're so beautiful," I said.

She made a face, but I pressed on.

"It's just — I don't know why you keep it hidden."

Hel sighed and turned to the wall, showing me her left side. It must be a reflex, I realized, showing her impassive skeletal side anytime someone provokes a reaction.

"Hel, you're the most beautiful woman in the Nine Realms."

"And that's all I would be," she said.

"Excuse me?"

She took a deep breath. Her hands were knotting the blanket around her chest. "My mother started my marriage negotiations before I could walk," she said. "She had a lot to gain by a prosperous alliance, and even more to gain playing my suitors off one another. By the time I turned ten, my whole life was laid out for me."

I nodded. My life followed a similar path, although I wasn't betrothed to Nanna until I turned eighteen. Still, it's not like I had a say in the whole arrangement.

"So...it was your way of avoiding marriage?"

She sighed again. "No. Yes, but no."

"It's okay. If I'm pressing my bounds as your consort, just tell me."

"It wasn't just marriage, though. It was everything. I mean, what do you know of Freyja?"

"What do you mean?"

Hel rolled her eyes. "She's beautiful, right?"

"Well, of course. But I know she has her chariot, and her share of the dead from Midgard. And her necklace."

"Right. But before all that, above all that: She's beautiful. That's what Freyja is, right? Beautiful. And I didn't want to be that. I didn't want to be reduced."

I frowned, trying to understand. "I don't think Freyja feels like she's been, uh, reduced."

Hel shook her head, her fiery hair slowly settling over her shoulders. "If anyone could understand, I would think it would be you. Doesn't it ever bother you to be Baldr the Beautiful?"

"Well, I don't know..." I said, my voice fading as I considered her words.

Of course it got annoying. There were times when it would be nice to talk to someone without having them blush, or giggle, or pretend it was an accident when our bodies brushed together. But it was damned useful, too. To give that up, to have to get by just on the strength of my personality..? I shivered.

"When did you start?" I asked.

Hel straightened her back. "My father taught me illusions on my thirteenth birthday."

I whistled. "And that was it? You just kept wearing it?"

"Pretty much." She shrugged. "Everyone who'd known me before assumed it was some kind of a curse. My mother knew, of course, but she couldn't say. It would have been too embarrassing to reveal she couldn't control me. And the suitors just disappeared. Eventually."

I walked to the bed and kissed the back of her neck, then sat in front of her and kissed her forehead. "Then I feel incredibly lucky you've chosen to share yourself with me."

Her smile lit her eyes and, before she could respond, my lips were on hers, my hands moving over the irresistable curves of her body, pushing the covers away, rediscovering the glorious, hidden secrets of her body.

"YOU KEEP LOOKING AT me," Hel said, the corners of her mouth pulling into a shy smile.

It was the first time we'd left her chambers in days, and we were walking through the orchard. It was my idea. Since she surprised me with an enormous bed, and a couch to replace her lone, uncomfortable chair, there hadn't been much reason to leave her room. I'd joked Hel's subjects might all think I managed to abscond with her and, after she laughed, she told me it was probably time to show me off.

So we walked through the castle, arm in arm. I found it quite satisfying to watch the horrified expressions in our wake. After all my many years of trying to please everyone, I found it inordinately satisfying to make people uncomfortable. And then, once we'd said hello to what I imagined had to be every single person in the castle, I asked to come back here, to the place where I'd first seen her without her illusion.

The blossoms were slightly past their prime. Only a few white flowers lined the branches, and most of the petals lay in heaps and drifts on the grass. Another rumpled stray petal had managed to find its way into the fiery golden curls of Hel's hair. She'd shed her illusion once she felt certain we were alone, and the sunlight only highlighted her unearthly beauty.

"I don't think I'll ever be able to stop looking at you," I said.

She smiled, but Hel wasn't one to be put off by flattery. "You're looking at me like you have a question," she said.

I grinned. I did, in fact, have a question.

"It's this place," I began. "It made you uncomfortable, the first time we came here. I just wondered why."

She frowned and turned, showing the left side of her face.

"You don't have to tell me," I said.

"No, it's fine," she said, waving her hand. "I guess it's just embarrassing."

I took her hand, kissed it, and waited.

"I love these orchards," she said, her voice soft as the flower petals at our feet. "They're the most beautiful place in Niflhel. And I suppose, when I brought you here, I was trying to impress you." Her cheeks flared red.

"It worked," I said.

Hel shook her head. "It was more than that, though. I mean, I knew I couldn't hope to impress Baldr the Beautiful, the most attractive man in the Nine Realms. It was hopeless to even try. So I was upset with myself for making such a stupid, misguided attempt."

I pulled her into my arms, folding her soft warmth against my chest. "And yet you did impress me."

She sighed, her body relaxing against mine. I kissed her hair and stared at the trees, the rows and rows of thick, gnarled trunks that must have been lovingly pruned year after year. They had to be ancient. My heart ached as a new thought broke through my consciousness.

"Hel, did you plant this orchard?"

She nodded against my chest. "Of course. I took cuttings from Jötunheimr. I loved the orchards there."

I felt cold. The hundreds of years these trees had seen, the flood of time it must have taken to grow an orchard from a cutting. Years upon years of wearing an illusion, hiding her true self. Walking alone through the flower blossoms each spring.

"All that time," I said, "and you never took another consort?"

She laughed, but it was a small, sad laugh. "You know what I look like. You really think anyone else would be crazy enough to want me?"

I kissed her hair, then her ear. "You could have shown him this," I whispered, moving my lips along the hollow of her collarbone, the place that always made her gasp.

"No, I couldn't. I..."

Her words trailed off as my hand moved down her backside, undoing the clasps of her dress.

"Oh, Hel," I moaned, running my face along her neck as I slipped the dress off her shoulders. "We have got so much time to make up."

She moaned and pressed her hips into mine. My cock surged in response, hungry for her. Her fingers traced the bulge in my pants and it was my turn to gasp, to press my body into her touch.

A trumpet sounded, the clear note rising across the orchard, shaking the blossoms on the trees. Hel backed away and her body stiffened in a flurry of light as she wove her illusion. By the time she'd pulled her dress back over her shoulders, we heard the thud of horse's hooves and Eriksen's voice.

"Hel!" he called. "Hel, are you here?"

"Yes," she responded, hiding none of her irritation.

A moment later Eriksen's enormous black stallion crashed through the trees, scattering petals and twigs in its wake. He dismounted, bowing low before Hel. "I am so sorry."

She crossed her arms over her chest. "I specifically asked not to be disturbed."

"Yeah, what if we'd been otherwise occupied?" I added.

Eriksen shuddered as I grinned at him.

"I would never have come if the situation hadn't warranted my actions," he said stiffly.

Hel sighed. "Fine. What's the situation?"

Eriksen hesitated, his eyes darting over me before returning to Hel. "It's... It is a bit delicate."

"Anything you have to say to me can be said in the presence of my consort."

"Very well. Queen Hel, Frigg has traveled to Niflhel."

I shuddered as if I'd been hit. "What? My mother Frigg?"

Hel's hand wrapped gently around my wrist. "Has she died?"

"No. No, she is very much alive. And she is, uh, demanding to speak with you."

Hel frowned. "About what?"

Eriksen's eyes jumped over me again. "About him. I believe she is going to request the return of Baldr."

CHAPTER EIGHT

IT WAS ONLY THE SECOND time I'd seen the throne room, and it was far more intimidating this time around. The torches cast flickering orange light across the hard, black walls and floor. Even the crowd looked somber, dressed in dark colors with serious expressions.

And Hel looked, well, terrifying. She wore all black, and the torches highlighted the harsh white lines of her exposed skeleton. Her human side was no more welcoming than her dead side, with her pale lips set in a hard line. She wore no crown and held no scepter. She didn't need to. Her nightmare body on her ebony throne said it all.

Hel suggested I wait in the shadows until we understood exactly what my mother was doing in the realm of the inglorious dead, so I missed Frigg's approach. I heard the ripple of subdued conversation, the rustle of clothing as people turned to watch her walk through the room. I sank back in the crowd, trying not to make eye contact.

It was only once the low ebb of conversation ceased entirely and the crowd stood still that I was able to see my mother, standing tall in front of the throne. I had to admit, Frigg looked pretty terrifying herself. She wore her full robes, with the heavy silver crown she almost never brought out of the vault. There was a hard line between her eyebrows that I'd learned to fear as a child. Her servant Fulla stood behind her, along with my brother Hermod. Shrewd. Traveling to Niflhel alone would have been unwise, but a woman accompanied by her servant and son were hardly enough to be considered an invasion. Although they would be quite formidable, if it came to fighting.

Hel raised her skeletal hand and the crowd shifted, craning to view the throne.

"Queen Frigg," Hel began, her voice as cold as the black stone walls. "How rare to have a visit from the realms of the living. To what do I owe the honor?"

My mother inclined her head very, very slightly. "Queen Hel. I'll not waste your time with unnecessary formalities. I have come for Baldr Óðinnsen. I will return him to Asgard, and we shall leave you in peace."

My heart sank. We knew what she'd demand, of course. Still, I'd held onto some small, wild hope she was here for another reason.

Hel arched her delicate dark eyebrow. "Why?"

A ripple of subdued conversation moved across the room. I saw the edge of Frigg's mouth twitch. She hadn't expected that response.

"Excuse me?" Frigg asked.

"Baldr Óðinnsen died," Hel said. "As he did not fall in battle, he belongs to my realm. And yet here you are, demanding I violate the rules of all Nine Realms by returning him to Asgard. Why would I do such a thing?"

"He belongs in Asgard," Frigg said.

"He's dead," Hel answered. "He belongs here."

The line between Frigg's eyes deepened. "He is one of the Æsir. His home is Asgard."

"Perhaps you should be having this conversation with your husband," Hel replied. "Is Óðinn not the one who established the borders between the living and the dead?"

Frigg scowled. Even as a grown man, that expression terrified me.

"Baldr is essential to Asgard," she said. "He belongs to us, and I am going to take him back."

"Perhaps we should ask Baldr," Hel said casually, her eyes flickering over me.

The crowd turned to watch as I emerged from the shadows. Frigg's lower lip quivered for a heartbeat, before she raised her hand to hide her mouth. I bowed before her, then turned and bowed before Hel.

"My son!" Frigg embraced me, and my heart clenched. She smelled good, warm and soft despite her formal robes.

"Hi, Mom." I took a deep breath as we pulled apart. "It's good to see you."

She wiped her eyes. "My dear, I've come to take you home."

The room was silent. Her voice echoed strangely off the walls. Home. Funny how that word already sounded odd on her lips.

"Mom. I am home."

Frigg frowned, then raised her hand and waved it slowly in front of my face. My body tingled with her magic as she searched for an enchantment.

I shook my head. "Look, you can see I'm not enchanted. Mom, I've spent a lifetime serving you and my father. I've done everything you requested, wooed whomever you needed to impress. And now it's over."

"Your wife and child mourn you," she said.

"I know. I'm sorry. But my time in Asgard has ended."

"Your poor wife's heart is broken, Baldr! Nanna almost threw herself on your funeral pyre!"

I winced. "But she didn't, did she, Mom?"

Frigg's lips pressed into a tight line. She had to know how little love there was between me and Nanna. She straightened her shoulders and turned away, dismissing me entirely.

"You must love him very much," Frigg said to Hel, "to create such a convincing doppelgänger."

Anger surged through me, hot and immediate. "Damn it, Mom, listen to me! I'm not enchanted, and I'm not a doppelgänger—"

Hel raised her hand, and I fell silent. Of course it was futile. Frigg and Óðinn never cared what I wanted when I was alive. Why would they care now that I was dead?

"I wonder where my real son actually is," Frigg said, raising her voice so it carried throughout the entire throne room. "Is he in your chambers, Queen Hel? Do you force him to warm your bed?"

A low murmur spread through the crowd, and I clenched my fists. I knew my mother would take that as all the proof she needed.

Frigg smiled, and her tone warmed. "Queen Hel, please don't think me cruel. I do understand. Baldr is beautiful as the sun. All Nine Realms love him. It's only natural you would love him too."

Hel remained motionless, her face carefully neutral.

"But, my Queen," Frigg continued, "should your love for Baldr cancel the love of all the living realms? Surely you can see he belongs to the living. We all love him, Hel. We love him more than you possibly could."

Hel frowned. "And here I thought you wanted Baldr back because he was useful."

Frigg nodded. "He is useful, Queen Hel. Baldr's good looks open many doors for us."

I shivered. I'd always known my parents used me in their political machinations, but I'd never heard it put quite so bluntly before.

"The peace and goodwill my son spreads to the realms help us all," Frigg said, spreading her arms as if she were including the inglorious dead in her statement. "Weigh that against the needs of your bedchamber, Queen Hel."

Frigg drew herself up tall. "And, if you dare ask for my real son's opinion, think of where he'd rather be. In Asgard he has his pick of romantic companions from across the living realms. But here..." She let her voice trail off as she glanced around the room. The crowd shifted uncomfortably.

Hel raised her skeletal hand and the murmurs stopped. "Enough. You say everyone loves your son? All the living realms?"

"They do, my Queen. You know it is true."

"Prove it."

Frigg's brow furrowed. "Excuse me?"

"If everyone loves Baldr the Beautiful, then everyone will mourn him, no?"

Frigg's mouth opened, closed, opened again. "But of course. We all mourn him."

The corner of Hel's living lip curved in the smallest suggestion of a smile. "Then prove it. If everyone, and I mean every living, sentient being across the realms, wails in torment over Baldr's death, then I shall return him to Asgard."

Everyone gasped. Including me.

"But." Hel raised her hand again. "If there is so much as one creature who does not shed a tear, your son remains in Niflhel. Forever."

Frigg blinked. She looked pale in the torchlight.

"Do we have a deal?" Hel asked, in a voice as fearsome as her appearance.

"I-Yes. Yes, Queen Hel. I agree to your terms." Frigg inclined her head slightly and then turned, sweeping from the room without waiting to be dismissed. Fulla and Hermod scurried after her. My brother tried to catch my eye as we left, but I ignored him. I ignored them all.

I was looking at Hel.

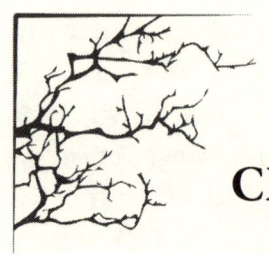

CHAPTER NINE

HEL'S LIVING HAND CLENCHED her throne so tightly her knuckles had turned white. Her dark hair trembled against her neck. I jumped onto the dais and was at her side by the time she stood. I opened my mouth, but she shook her head, silencing me. I followed her, waiting as she walked from her throne and through the halls, answering a ceaseless stream of questions from various advisors. When I tried to hold her hand, she pulled away from my touch.

I half expected her to slam the door to her chambers in my face, but she motioned for me to enter before pulling the heavy door closed.

"What the fuck was that?" I said, finally breaking my silence as she slid the oak bar across her door, locking us in.

"Shut up," she snapped.

"You're the queen," I said. "You could have just said no."

She shook her head as the radiance of golden light enveloped her body, obscuring her features. By the time the light faded, Hel was halfway undressed.

"You could have sent Frigg away," I said.

Hel ignored me, pushing her robes down the generous swell of her hips. It was almost enough to distract me.

"Why did you do it?" I insisted.

She stepped out of her robes and wrapped her arms around my neck. "Shut up, Baldr."

"Making a bargain with Frigg? Don't you think that's just a little bit risky?"

"Damn it, you're not my advisor!" she snapped. Her hips rocked into mine and my body responded to her heat, my cock stiffening against the seam of my pants.

"But—"

Hel pressed her lips to mine, kissing me with an angry hunger. I opened to her, letting her tongue claim me as her hands ran through my hair and slipped up my shirt. The air filled with the sweet tang of her arousal as she rubbed against me.

"Shut up, Baldr," she hissed against my skin. "Shut up and do what you're here for."

I bit off a moan. In all my long years, no woman had ever said anything like that to me before. Damn, it turned me on.

"What I'm here for?" I growled.

Hel's hands were already fumbling with my belt. I reached down and helped her, pushing my pants over my hips. My cock sprang out, searching for her heat. I grabbed her ass and lifted her, shoving her against the cold wall of her bedchamber.

"Is this what I'm here for?" I asked, nipping the skin below her ear.

Hel moaned. Heat poured off her body, and I pressed my cock against her wet folds. She was so hot, so ready.

"Is this what you want?"

"Oh, Baldr," she moaned.

"You want this cock?" I growled, holding myself just outside her cunt, feeling her entire body tremble in my arms.

"Yes! Yes, please, yes!"

I thrust inside her. She gasped, her eyes opening wide and then closing in pleasure. I shoved her against the wall, fucking her hard and fast, losing myself in her heat, her smell, the softness of her body. Oh, this woman did it for me! Her body tightened around my cock as she gasped with each thrust, arching her back against the wall, driving me deeper and deeper. I growled as our sweat poured together, energy sparking and arcing between our bodies. She was the most gorgeous woman I'd ever seen, the most gorgeous woman in the Nine Realms and, in this moment, she was mine.

I didn't expect her to come, but suddenly she was screaming, her body clenching around my cock, her nails digging into the skin of my back. I froze, pressing her against the wall as she shook and rippled under me. I drank her in, watching her beautiful face tilt back, her eyes closed and her lips parted as pleasure burned through her.

Oh, damn. It hurt, but I made myself stop. I bit the inside of my mouth and pulled back as she collapsed against my shoulder. My legs were trembling by now, but I picked her up and spun, sitting her on the table.

She blinked and raised her head. "Baldr?"

"Lie down, Queen. I am nowhere near finished with you."

She sighed and lay back, her golden hair flowing across the parchment strewn over her desk. I grabbed her hips and pulled her to the edge of the table, teasing her pussy with the head of my cock. When she moaned I had to take a deep breath, focusing.

"Not that," I hissed.

Hel had enough time to give me a confused frown before I grabbed her thighs and pulled her over.

"Oh," she whispered, her cheeks flushing as her feet found the floor. I ran my hand along her back, pushing her down against the desk.

Damn, what an ass! I traced her thighs with my fingertips, watching her skin shiver under my touch. Her pussy was glistening wet, and she whimpered when I pressed my cock against her folds. I entered her slowly, teasing her as she shivered beneath me, running my hands along the curve of her perfect ass as I stared at her body spread out before me, her fiery hair plastered to her back, her eyes closed as she moaned for me. Oh, she was exquisite with that ass in the air, flushed a delicate pink. I couldn't resist. I pulled back my hand and brought it down on her backside, smacking her. She gasped as her body tightened around my cock.

I reached forward, digging my hands into her long hair. "You like that?" I growled.

"I-oh, I..." she panted, her hips rocking back against mine.

I smacked her again, this time hard enough to leave a red mark on her creamy skin.

"Oh! Yes!" she yelped.

"You are a harlot," I said, pulling back on her hair. "You're my harlot."

Her body rippled under me, grasping my cock and pushing me closer to the edge. "Say it," I growled.

"I'm yours!" She cried. "I'm your harlot!"

"Damn right you are." I smacked her again, hard.

"I'm yours, Baldr! I'm-I'm...oh!"

She screamed, and her entire body clenched around mine. I thrust into her as she came, lifting her off the ground, exploding inside her, my orgasm ripping through me like fire, like lightning, leaving me trembling and panting.

I collapsed on top of her, pressing our bodies together. "My Queen," I whispered, still gasping for breath, "I am nowhere near done with you."

She sighed. It sounded like *yes*.

I FUCKED HER HARD THAT night, in every way I could imagine. When I'd come so many times I started to seriously doubt my ability to ever have another hard-on in my life, I bent over and licked my seed out of her until she screamed my name as her body spasmed under my lips. It was so irresistibly sexy I found I could indeed screw her again.

I didn't want to admit it, not even to myself, but I was terrified. Frigg was the woman who traveled all Nine Realms, after all, making everything vow not to harm me. She was dangerously single-minded; if anyone could make the living realms cry, it would be my mother.

And if we lost, if Frigg somehow managed to make all the living realms cry for me, my separation from Hel would be permanent. It was only a stupid oversight that got me here in the first place. When she made all creation swear not to harm me, Frigg forgot mistletoe. And I was damned certain that little omission had been corrected.

If I were hauled back to Asgard, there would be nothing in the Nine Realms capable of killing me. I'd be trapped in the land of the living, and Hel would be in the land of the dead.

Forever.

So I fucked her hard, fucked her until she screamed and screamed. I wanted to make sure Hel's next consort had a tough act to follow.

CRY. MAKING THE REALMS cry.

I emerged from the hazy world of my dreams slowly. I'd been dreaming about crying, somehow. And even now it seemed I could hear the muffled sound of someone sobbing. I shifted in the bed, rubbing my eyes. Hel huddled in the blankets on the far side of the bed. Crying.

I sat up. Hel had pulled the blanket over her head, and her entire body rocked back and forth with her muffled sobs.

"Hey, hey, hey," I said, reaching for her.

She pulled the blanket tighter.

"It's okay, it's me. It's Baldr."

Her grip relaxed and I pulled the blanket down. She gasped through her sobs. Her eyes were swollen and red, and her cheeks were streaked with tears.

She was so beautiful it almost hurt to look at her.

"Here, sit up. It's okay, Hel. It's okay."

I pulled her upright and glanced around the darkened room, trying to find something to drink. Mead would be good. Akvavit would be better. But all I saw was a graceful black carafe of water. I poured a glass and offered it to her, rubbing her back until she calmed down enough to open her lips and take a tiny swallow.

"I swear, Hel, I'm going to get some akvavit for this room," I said.

Her lips curled for a heartbeat. "I can't drink," she whispered. "It makes the illusion...more difficult."

I kissed her damp cheek, pushing her hair behind her ear as I wrapped my arm around her shoulders. "Do you want to tell me what's wrong?"

She trembled, and for a second I thought she'd start crying again. Instead she sighed and wiped her eyes.

"She's right, you know."

"Who's right?" I asked.

"Your mother. She's right, damn it." Her voice cracked and I refilled the water glass, giving her a moment to collect herself.

She wouldn't meet my eyes when I sat down next to her.

"All the realms do love you. And the way I feel for you, what is that to them? She's right." Her voice hitched and another tear slid down her cheek. "I can't compete with every woman in the living realms."

"Oh, stop it." I kissed her cheek. "There's no competition. No one could compete with you."

Hel shook her head. "No. Thanks, but she's still right. My needs can't outweigh the love of everyone in the living realms. I'm selfish, keeping you here."

"Damn it, Hel, that's not true. What you want matters. What I want matters. And I want to be with you."

Hel pulled her hands away and hid her face, her shoulders shaking.

"Shhhh, it's okay," I murmured, pulled her into my arms. "Look, beautiful, it'll never work anyway. There's no way Frigg can make everyone cry."

Hel sniffed. "Really?"

I forced myself to smile. "Really. You think people who've never even met me are going to cry for me? Please. It'll never work."

HEL PUT HER MUG OF tea down on the ebony table and stared out across the flat shine of the river, the dead side of her face revealing nothing.

"I couldn't refuse Frigg," she whispered.

I raised an eyebrow and leaned closer. She had been especially quiet this morning, even for her. Hel took the news about Midgard hard, although I hadn't been particularly surprised to hear all the mortals cried.

It had been just over a month since Frigg traveled to Niflhel, demanding my return. Of course the Æsir of Asgard cried for me, or at least the ones Frigg could round up, although I noticed Hel's father Loki was conspicuously absent from the lists of Æsir who'd cried.

And of course the mortals of Midgard cried for Frigg. They would do anything for Frigg. Or, more accurately, they'd do anything for a representative of Óðinn.

But now Frigg was traveling to Álfheim, home of the Light-elves, the arrogant victors of their little civil war. Those elves were vicious and aloof, nothing like the gullible mortals of Midgard, and they had no particular respect for Óðinn's leadership.

Frigg's little mission would end in Álfheim. I could feel it.

"And why couldn't you refuse Frigg?" I asked.

Hel sighed, staring at her hands. "Because she's Óðinn's wife."

"Yes, that much I knew."

She didn't even smile. "Baldr, Óðinn is the one who gave me this throne."

"Ah." I leaned back in my chair.

"If I refused his request, or his wife's request..."

"He could take back the throne," I said. "I'm so sorry."

She turned to me, frowning. "Sorry for what?"

"I accused you of being unwise for making that deal. I was an idiot. Slamming the door in Frigg's face could have sparked a war, or gotten you deposed. But a bargain..."

Hel smiled for the first time since Frigg traveled to Midgard to make the mortals cry. "And Óðinn's wife herself agreed to the deal."

I reached across the table and grabbed her hand. "You're brilliant, you know."

Her living cheek colored with a slight blush, but her frown deepened. "It hasn't worked yet."

"But it will! Come on now, Frigg's up against the Light-elves. You know they have no love for the Æsir. You think they give two shits about me, or my illustrious parents, in Álfheim?"

She giggled and looked at me with such desperate hope my heart broke. "You think so?"

I leaned across the table to kiss her forehead. "Of course, beautiful."

Someone coughed behind us, and I turned to see Eriksen standing stiffly by the door. He nodded to me and bowed to Hel.

"The advisors are ready," he said.

Shit. His voice was heavy and formal. Not a good sign.

"Very well," Hel said, coming to her feet. "Let's get this over with."

I walked with Hel and Eriksen through the maze of narrow hallways and to the small conference room. Ever since Frigg's arrival in Niflhel, I'd been attending the meetings with Hel's advisors. At first they looked somewhat askance at me, especially Eriksen, but after the first few days they started to smile and nod. After the first week, they even began to listen to what I had to say. It was a new experience, speaking without the weight of Óðinn's authority behind me, and being dismissed or lauded solely on the merit of my ideas.

And I liked it.

Which meant I now had even more to lose than the most beautiful woman in the Nine Realms, should Frigg's plan succeed and send me, kicking and screaming, back to the halls of Asgard.

Hel sat down first, followed by me and her advisors. They were all avoiding our eyes. Another bad sign.

"Go ahead," said Hel. I admired her self-control; she may as well have been talking about the weather.

Eriksen and Ganglati glanced at each other, then at Vigdis, the youngest member of Hel's council. She was usually the most cheerful face in the room, but this morning she looked miserable.

"Uh, Hel," Vigdis said, pushing back from the table. "I've, um, I've got our first report from Álfheim."

"Please continue," said Hel.

"Well, it sounds like Frigg, uh, she brought Bragi with her. To Álfheim. And he played a new song."

I groaned. Damn Bragi and his stupid, overwrought, emotional music.

"Is that all?" Hel asked.

Vigdis bit her lip and turned to me. "Not quite. Nanna Nepsdóttir went with them too. She's Baldr's, um, wife—"

"Yes, I know who Nanna is," Hel snapped. "Just tell me what happened."

Vigdis took a deep breath. "They cried, my Queen. I'm so sorry. Nanna and Frigg sang Bragi's song, and the Light-elves cried."

CHAPTER TEN

THEY ALL CRIED.

First the Light-elves, and then the Vanir of Vanaheimr, and then the dwarves and dark-elves of Svartálfaheimr. Even the demons of Múspell cried for me. Entire realms full of people who'd never met me sobbed over my death.

I'd been reduced to an idea, an abstract concept. Baldr the Beautiful. The Lost Son.

Perhaps, I thought in the long, indigo hours of the night, when I stood next to the window so my tossing and turning would not disturb Hel, I had always been an idea. The beautiful son of Óðinn and Frigg, softer and kinder than either of them. The shining, radiant, public face of Asgard, spreading peace and love throughout the realms. At least until the rest of the Æsir brought war.

I shivered and rubbed my arms, although the room wasn't cold. Hel broke down crying again last night, and it was all I could do to keep from despairing with her. Six of the seven living Realms had cried for me. And yesterday, Frigg, Bragi, and Nanna traveled to the very last of the living realms, the frozen wastes of Jötunheimr. I took a deep breath and ran my hand through my hair. The Jötunn hate the Æsir. It would be ridiculous to think they would cry over my death.

Wouldn't it?

I worried my lower lip and glanced at the bed. Hel was sleeping on her side, the covers pulled up to her chin. Her hair spread over the pillow like molten fire. She looked happier and more relaxed now, in the oblivion of sleep, than she'd been in days.

My stomach clenched and tears bit behind my eyelids. I brought my fist to my mouth, biting my knuckle. I didn't want to break down and start sobbing myself. I needed to stay strong for Hel, to comfort her. To be her consort.

Besides, Jötunheimr wouldn't cry.

They couldn't.

"WHAT HAPPENED TO THE apples?" I asked.

Hel was despondent when she woke this morning, so I asked if we could go for a walk in the orchard, hoping I could coax a smile from her in her favorite place. But the skies of Niflhel were low and gray today, and the grass was covered with small, hard fruits that had fallen from the trees. I fervently hoped that didn't mean these trees were dying, because losing her beloved orchard would do absolutely nothing to improve Hel's mood.

Hel shook her head. We were alone, but she was still wearing her illusion.

"It's normal," she said, in a voice that sounded like a sigh. "It's called early drop. The trees shed their smaller, weaker fruit early in the season. We make jelly with them, so it's not like anything is wasted."

I reached for her, running my finger along her chin. "That's better. You sound more like yourself when you're lecturing me."

She turned away, staring very intently at one of the trees. I followed her gaze to a small cluster of four tiny, green apples.

"These still look delicious," I murmured, wrapping my arms around her waist and pressing my lips to her neck.

"It's not like you'll be here to taste them," she snapped, pulling away.

"I didn't mean—"

I bit my tongue and held up my hands to let her go. She walked away, her body shivering with golden light beneath the heavy skies. I felt like crying. The weight of a thousand tears pressed against my shoulders, all the grief of the living bearing down on me, filling the space between my body and the lips and breasts and curves of this amazing woman, pushing us further and further apart.

I shook my head, trying to pull myself together as I followed her. She stood with her back rigid, facing the jagged black mountains. I walked behind her, raising my hands to cup the gentle curves of her shoulders.

"I'm sorry," I whispered.

Her shoulders slumped. "Me too."

"I don't want to lose you," I said, pressing my fingers into the tense muscles at the base of her neck. "But it's not over yet."

Hel gave an exasperated sort of huff. "I can't tell if you're trying to make me feel better, or if you really are the most stupidly optimistic person in the Nine Realms."

"Well, you did call me an idiot."

The living side of her mouth curled into a smile and, for a moment, she relaxed against my chest. But then her brow furrowed and she pulled away.

"Tell me you can see how hopeless this all is," she said.

My gut twisted. Hel was in pain, and I could do nothing to help, and it killed me. Watching her suffer was worse than suffering myself.

Damn it, I loved this woman. I loved her so much it hurt.

And telling her would only make everything worse.

"Things look pretty bad," I admitted, not wanting to lie to her. "But if I am going to lose you, Hel, I don't want to spend our last days together fighting."

She sighed and pressed the heels of her palms against her eyes. "Baldr, I should tell you—"

The great bell of Hel's castle tolled across the orchard, its echoing reverberations shaking the little green fruits.

"It's time," Hel said, pulling her back up straight. "They must have the report from Jötunheimr."

I forced myself to smile as I took her hand.

Until I was ripped from her side, I would do everything I could to bring her pleasure.

ERIKSEN STOOD OUTSIDE the meeting room, his eyes downcast. He opened the door without a word.

The advisors all came to their feet.

"Hel, Baldr," Ganglati said, nodding to both of us. "I'm so sorry."

My heart dropped and I turned to Hel, ready to wrap her in my arms. Her face betrayed nothing, but her grip on my hand tightened.

"Jötunheimr cried," Hel said. Her voice was cold and hollow, as if she were sitting on her throne.

Ganglati nodded, biting her lip. "Our reports are incomplete. And, of course, their sweeps haven't even begun. But it looks like the cities of Thrymheim and Útgarðar cried at Bragi's song, and that's almost the entire population of Jötunheimr."

"Even Angrboða?" Hel asked.

"Yes."

I flinched. Angrboða was Hel's mother.

"Leave us," Hel said. Her voice trembled slightly. "Please. All of you. Leave."

I pulled her into my arms and kissed her forehead. Her shoulders shook in my embrace. Two months ago her advisors would have recoiled, horrified to see someone touching Hel's rotting, skeletal body.

Now they shook their heads and gave me small, sympathetic smiles as they filed out. I even saw a few glistening eyes.

Great. More tears for Baldr.

Only when the door behind us closed did Hel let herself cry. Her illusion fell apart in my arms, collapsing in a shimmer of golden sparks, and I held her beautiful body as close as I could, trying to memorize her curves, her smell, her soft weight against my chest.

I cried. I couldn't help it, although I wiped my eyes and tried to smile when she pulled away.

"My dear Baldr," she said, taking my hands in hers. "I never thanked you. You gave me another life. You taught me so much about myself, about pleasure, about trust. Baldr, I—"

Her voice narrowed and choked off, drown in another wave of tears. I wrapped my arms around her. She was amazing, this gorgeous, fascinating woman. My mind wandered to her mother, Angrboða, who'd known how beautiful Hel truly was and tried to profit off it. Who betrayed her daughter by crying for Frigg. What kind of parent—

Parents.

My mind surged with sudden, desperate hope. Hel had another parent.

"Loki," I said. Hel's back straightened and I grabbed her chin, meeting her eyes. "Your father! Hel, he hasn't cried for Frigg!"

Her brow furrowed. "I thought he did. In Asgard."

"No, he didn't. They didn't reach all of the Æsir. He wasn't in any of the reports, remember? Can you contact him?"

Her eyes widened for a moment. "Yes, but... Baldr, my father isn't exactly helpful."

"I don't care! He's a chance. Let me talk to him!"

Her mouth opened, closed, opened again. "I-I don't...Oh, Baldr! What if you're right?"

She straightened her back and her body lit with golden fire as she wove her illusion before pulling the door open and taking off, almost running down the black stone hallways of her palace. I followed her for a long time, always heading down, until she took me to a narrow, twisting staircase I was certain I'd never seen before.

At the bottom was a heavily reinforced door with multiple locks. It swung open soundlessly at the touch of Hel's hand. Torches flickered on the damp stone walls of a circular room. There was a black pool in the floor. It refracted the light strangely, making the hairs on my neck prickle.

"Father," Hel said, her voice echoing. "I wish to speak."

The surface of the pool stirred and glimmered. I stared as the dark water grew lighter, becoming grey and then white, like mist. The mist swirled and parted, revealing a figure.

I blinked. Loki stood above the pool. Completely naked.

"Hello, daughter," he said. "So. How are you?"

Hel frowned. "Are you truly that oblivious, or are you just being an asshole?"

"Now, now, no need for that. You caught me at a delicate time, as you can no doubt see." He gestured to his body, turning his hips in a very distracting way. As always, Loki the Lie-smith was disarmingly handsome. I typically prefer women but, like almost all of the other Æsir, I'd enjoyed the occasional fling with Loki.

Probably something I won't mention to his daughter.

"I'm sorry," Hel muttered, staring at her feet. "I...I need your help. Father."

Loki laughed. "Oh, please don't tell me this is about Baldr. Just let the poor boy come home."

I watched a delicate flush spread across Hel's right cheek. "It's not that simple," she said.

"How unlike you to lose your head over a pretty face," Loki said. "But I suppose you're hardly the first. Just chalk it up to another afterlife learning experience and release him. The Æsir will be grateful, and they're not a bad bunch to have in your debt."

Hel's eyes flickered over me. The spark of hope had gone out; they were as dark and empty as the pool had been when we entered the room.

I pushed past her to stand in front of Loki.

"I don't want to return," I said.

Loki frowned, then looked over my shoulder to Hel. "Enchantment? Really? That's stooping a bit low, don't you think?"

Hel scowled. "How typically condescending of you, Father."

"Damn it, I'm not enchanted!" I yelled.

Loki turned back to me. His eyes widened.

"I don't want to return to Asgard," I said. "I'm done serving as Óðinn's errand boy."

"So you'd rather be dead?" Loki asked, arching an eyebrow.

"I'd rather be here, with your daughter." I took Hel's hand in mine. "I love her."

Hel gasped and I turned to her, running my hand along her left cheek, feeling her smooth skin beneath the skeletal illusion.

"Oh, Baldr! I love you, too. I've been trying to tell you—"

I kissed her, feeling her soft lips against mine. The room filled with golden light as her illusion vanished.

Loki snorted. "I suppose a beautiful woman is the oldest enchantment of all. Well, you two are totally fucked. So, if you'll excuse me..."

"Loki. Wait," I said, meeting his eyes.

I was the negotiator for Óðinn, the representative of Asgard. I held the peace across the Nine Realms for a thousand years. I should have been able to think of something to say to convince the Lie-smith to help us.

"Please." My voice was rough and pinched. "Please. Help us."

Loki rolled his eyes and shrugged his shoulders. "Fine. I'll do what I can."

The torches on the wall flared, and he vanished. I frowned at the oily surface of the pool.

"Does that mean he's going to do something, or not?" I asked, turning to Hel.

For the first time in days, Hel's smile reached her bright, sparkling eyes. "He'll do it," she said. "He's going to help. Oh, Baldr, thank you!"

I DIDN'T EXPECT TO sleep that night, but I did. With my body pressed against Hel's soft curves and my face buried in her golden hair, I slept better than I'd slept since Frigg's deal with Hel threatened everything.

But my dreams were dark and ominous. I woke with my heart pounding, trying to shake my feeling of being chased. Hel lay beside me, her chest rising and falling in sleep. I took a deep breath of her sweet, floral scent before sliding off the bed and pacing to the window.

The sky was just beginning to lighten, changing from ebony to indigo along the jagged edge of the far mountains. I'd slept the entire night, then. Surprising. I smiled at Hel's dark, quiet outline. Still sleeping. Good for her.

I slid the bar off the door as quietly as I could and slipped into the hallway. Most of the castle was still asleep, but the kitchen would be awake. I followed the twisting curves of the dark hallways to the feast hall, returning a few warm smiles from the handful of people already at the long wooden tables. I grabbed a popover and mug of tea from the kitchen, kissed the old cook on her wrinkled cheek, and found a quiet table.

"Baldr?"

I looked up to see Hel's advisor Ganglati, her forehead creased and her lips pressed together. My heart sunk.

"Have a seat," I said.

"Thanks." She pulled up a chair.

"What's the news?"

Ganglati shook her head. "Nothing good, I'm afraid. They've started sweeping Jötunheimr."

"Shit." My popover suddenly looked revolting. I pushed the plate away.

Sweeping was the last step in their plan. First Frigg, Bragi, and Nanna traveled to the major cities. They played in auditoriums, at fairs and festivals. They would make entire cities cry, filling the streets with weeping mortals, or dwarves, or Light-elves. And then, after making the cities cry together, they split up to cover the countryside. They knocked on the door of every damn shack in every damn realm, forcing everyone to hear their stupid sob story.

"How long do we have?" I asked, my stomach churning.

Ganglati shrugged. "Hard to say. Jötunheimr's a big realm. Maybe two weeks?"

I sighed. The good mood I'd had after our conversation with Loki was dissipating like morning fog hovering over the river. Ganglati grabbed my hand. She had dark circles under her eyes, almost like bruises. So I wasn't the only one finding it hard to sleep. Maybe that should have been comforting.

"Try to keep Hel happy," Ganglati said. "While you can."

"Yeah. I'll do my best."

Ganglati smiled. "We're glad you're here, Baldr."

I blinked and wiped my eyes with the back of my hand, trying to get a hold of myself as Ganglati walked away.

The last thing the realms needed was more tears.

CHAPTER ELEVEN

"COULD WE RUN AWAY?" I asked.

Hel curled against my chest, her hair spread over my arms. We'd come together over and over, with frantic desperation, until our bodies were completely spent. Still, sleep eluded both of us.

"Run to where?" she said, her voice muffled against the pillows.

"Another realm. Another underworld. Didn't you say you know another land of the dead?"

She shook her head. "It wouldn't work."

"Couldn't we hide somewhere? Together?"

Hel pulled away and turned, meeting my eyes in the dim flickers of torchlight. "And break my oath to Frigg? You'd make me just like my father."

I bit my lip. That one hurt. It had been almost two weeks since we spoke to Loki in the dark, subterranean pool. And so far, he'd apparently done jack fucking shit for us. It felt like the walls were closing in all around us. We needed a way out, something to break the oath Hel swore to Frigg. I sighed and sat up, staring at the sky outside Hel's windows. It was already growing lighter.

Death breaks all bonds, Ada said when I first arrived. But we're already dead. What could we possible do to—

My eyes fell to the steep slopes of the dark, jagged mountains.

"My Queen," I said. "If we fail, I would be delighted to accompany you to the darkness."

Hel jolted upright, her eyes widening. "But—"

"If death breaks all bonds, surely the darkness does the same?"

She frowned. "Perhaps. Baldr, I don't know. No one knows what happens when you join the darkness."

"So? Does it really matter? We know what will happen if we don't."

A subtle flash of golden light shimmered across her collarbone. We hadn't spoken of it, but yes, we both knew what we had to lose.

"And what if we just fall apart?" Hel said. "What if we're pulled to nothingness, like smoke?"

I smiled. "Then at least we would be pulled to nothingness together, my love."

"We may be born again, with no memories of who we once were."

"My love, if that happens, I will search the Nine Realms until I find you."

Hel snorted. "That's absurd, and you know it. With no memories how would we ever find each other?"

"I will find you."

"Oh, really? And if you're born a Light-elf and I'm the lowliest dwarf in Svartálfaheimr?"

I laughed. "Then it will be one hell of an epic romance. Just think of the songs Bragi could write about us."

Her lip twitched in the barest suggestion of a smile.

"The physical complications alone would probably be worth twenty stanzas," I said, watching her. "I mean, Light-elves are at least twice the size of dwarfs..."

Hel finally laughed and, for a heartbeat, the world stopped pressing in on top of us.

There was a sharp rap on the door. We both jumped.

"Hel?" Eriksen's muffled voice carried through the heavy door. "I apologize, but there is news you should hear. You should both hear it."

My heart plunged, and my body turned cold. Hel took my hand as our eyes met. Hers glinted like steel in the flickering torchlight.

"Yes," she whispered.

I shivered as I nodded in agreement. It was done, then. One way or another, I would not be returning to Asgard and the Æsir.

Hel rose, shivering with golden light as she re-wove her illusion after our sleepless night. I stood and pulled on my pants, feeling clumsy in comparison. Two weeks. That must have been enough time to finish the sweep of Jötunheimr, to knock on every hidden, forsaken hamlet and crofter's cottage and cave in the icy realm.

I felt numb. Frigg actually pulled it off. She'd make all the living realms cry for someone who never even existed; her mythical, perfect, beautiful son.

I had to die to lay some claim to my own life. And now I was about to lose that too.

Hel slid the bar off her door and nodded to Eriksen. The torch he held shivered slightly as she straightened her back and offered me her living arm. "Would you care to accompany me to the meeting with my advisors, my dear consort?" she asked.

I swallowed my desperation. "It would be my pleasure," I said, taking her arm in mine.

AS USUAL, HEL'S ADVISORS came to their feet when we entered the room, and they waited until we sat to take their places around the table. I saw a few smiles, which struck me as horribly inappropriate. Perhaps I'd misread their earlier acceptance? My stomach clenched. Well, if they'd only been tolerating me or humoring Hel, at least they wouldn't have to put up with me much longer.

I idly wondered which darkness Hel would choose. She'd told me most people prefer to cross the river and climb into the mountains, but I thought she might want to return to the asphodel fields. We could walk under those graceful birch trees together, arm in arm into the darkness.

No. First we'd make love, and then we would walk into oblivion. I wanted to see the rapture of orgasm play across her gorgeous face one more time. I turned to smile at Hel. She looked even paler than usual.

Hel cleared her throat as she faced her advisors. "You may begin," she said.

Ganglati stood, her eyes shining. "The sweep of Jötunheimr is almost complete. Yesterday they'd done all but the furthest Northern reaches, which would have been completed by this evening."

"Would have been?" Hel interrupted.

Ganglati nodded. "My Queen. Baldr. We've just gotten the latest report."

She paused. The room was so silent I could hear the distant murmur of early morning conversation in the feast hall.

"Someone refused to cry," Ganglati said.

I let out the breath I'd been holding since Frigg left Niflhel.

"Who?" Hel asked.

"An old woman named Tokk. She's a hermit, living in a remote valley. Frigg approached her alone yesterday at sunset. It sounds like she was there all night, but Tokk never cried. Apparently she told Frigg, 'Let Hel hold what she has.'"

Hel closed her eyes. Color rushed back into the living side of her face.

Ganglati cleared her throat. "There's more."

"Please," Hel said, waving her hand.

Ganglati and Eriksen exchanged a glance.

"Well, there are several among the Æsir who speculate that Tokk was actually, um, Loki the Lie-smith."

I saw the corner of Hel's mouth twitch as she crossed her hands on the table.

"Of course, we all know Loki couldn't openly defy Frigg and Óðinn," Ganglati continued.

Hel cleared her throat, cutting off Ganglati. "I don't really care what the Æsir speculate, or who Tokk may have been. We just won. The Æsir can think whatever they like."

She turned to Eriksen. "Would you be kind enough to deliver a message to Asgard? Please tell them we are aware of the Jötunn Tokk, and her refusal to cry for Baldr." She paused. "You can tell the Æsir that Hel will hold what she has."

"It would be my pleasure, my Queen." Eriksen beamed as he bowed low before Hel. Then he stood and turned to me. "And Baldr, please allow me be the first to say I'm glad you will remain in Niflhel."

I swallowed around the growing lump in my throat. "Thanks," I stammered.

The room filled with cheers and I turned to see Hel beaming, her eyes sparkling above her half smile. Even her skeletal side seemed radiant. My heart surged. I stood and pulled her to her feet, wrapping my arms around her and kissing her deeply. Hel's advisors clapped as our lips and tongues danced. Some distant part of my brain realized we'd have to think of new ways to shock them.

Hel pulled away gasping, a delicate golden shiver running down her neck and shoulders. I tightened my grip around her waist, not wanting to let her go. Not just yet. She tucked her hair behind her ear and turned back to her advisors.

"Thank you," she said. "Thank you all."

I followed her gaze, watching the smiles around the table. They truly liked Hel, I realized, and it was not a loyalty born of fear or hope for reward. No, it was more akin to love. She'd given me a new life, this fascinating, beautiful woman. She'd given us all a new life.

"If you'll excuse us," I said, grinning at the advisors, "I would appreciate a moment alone with the Queen."

I didn't wait to see their reactions. I pulled Hel to my chest, kissing her as I ran my fingers through her hair and down her back. Then I spun, pressing her against the smooth black table as the room emptied.

"Baldr," she gasped. "What are you doing?"

I grinned against her neck. "I've just received the best news of my entire afterlife. And if you think I'm going to wait one more second before fucking you senseless, my love, you are mistaken."

She moaned as the door slammed shut, giving us the room to ourselves. I bit her earlobe as I spread her legs, pushing the folds of her dress up along her thighs.

"This is the meeting room," she whispered, her voice already thick with arousal.

"Oh, I know. I don't even think that door locks. Someone could walk in at any moment."

A wave of heat poured off her, and the heady scent of her arousal filled the space between us. My cock pulsed, straining against the seam of my pants. I'd hoped taking her in this room would turn her on, and damn, I was glad to be proven right.

I wrapped one hand around her waist, pulling her to the edge of the table. Her body surged with light as I worked my pants down my thighs and ran my stiff cock along the wet slit of her sex.

"Concentrate," I said. "Hold your illusion."

She whimpered as I entered her, her back stiffening. She sank her fingers into my hair and her ankles crossed around my hips. For a heartbeat we held still, our bodies embracing, intertwined. The shimmers of light faded away, and her illusion held.

"Hel, you're amazing," I gasped.

I pulled back and reached between us, my fingers finding the hot swell of her clit, just above the place where our bodies came together. I watched her eyes roll back as I brushed it.

"Concentrate," I said as she moaned in my arms.

"Baldr!" she cried. Light filled the room, surging from her body in the same rhythm as my thrusts. "I can't!"

I squeezed her clit, rolling it between my fingers. "Yes, you can," I said.

Her body clenched around mine, tightening as it rolled with light. Still her illusion held; I was fucking Hel the fearsome, Hel the skeleton.

Damn, she was hot!

I slammed inside her, pressing her clit fast and hard. Her body felt so good in my arms, so damn good, I thought I might never let her go. She moaned my name over and over, her breath hot on my neck, her legs tight around my waist.

Hel screamed when she came, heat surging as her entire body closed around me. I watched her head rock back, her cheek and neck flushed crimson. A single drop of sweat trickled down the living side of her face.

Her illusion held.

She opened her eyes slowly, looking dazed. "I did it," she whispered.

I smiled as I started moving inside her again, slowly and deliberately. My fingers brushed her clit in a slow circle.

"Very nice," I panted. "But you didn't think we were done, did you?"

HEL'S ILLUSION SHATTERED entirely after her third orgasm. I hadn't expected her to hold the spell nearly that long. Honestly, I hadn't expected her to have that many orgasms in a row.

Once again, the Queen of Niflhel surprised me.

When she came a fourth time, I lost it. I'd tried so hard to hold out, to save myself and just keep pleasuring her, but the sight of that amazing woman lying across the black meeting table, the table where I'd heard so much terrible news over the past months, was just too much for me. I came hard inside her glorious body. It was like coming home, like surrender. Like dying.

I collapsed next to her, my head spinning. All I wanted was wrap her in my arms and hold her until the end of time. My mind started to unspool, drifting toward sleep.

But that damn door really didn't lock.

"Come on," I said, shaking myself awake.

Hel didn't resist as I pulled her to sitting, then to her feet. But she didn't let go of my arm once she stood, and it occurred to me she might not have anything left to spin her illusion.

"You think you can, uh, you know?" I stammered, waving my hand in the world's most pathetic attempt to describe magical illusions. "So we can go back to your bedchamber?"

She blinked, then smiled slowly at me. "Oh! Sure. Right."

Hel took a step forward and fell against my chest. When she started to giggle I worried she'd really lost it. I had a moment of panic when I considered wrapping her head in my shirt and carrying her through the halls. Then her body stiffened in my arms and familiar, warm light flooded the room. When I looked down, I was again holding Hel's half-dead form.

And she was still giggling.

"What's so damn funny?" I asked.

"Oh, Baldr," she sighed, rubbing her face against my neck. "I really think it's time for you to start calling it *our* bedchamber."

I kissed the top of her head and swept her into my arms, carrying her from the room. The few people we passed in the hallways of her castle were demure enough to turn away, and I doubt anyone noticed that the hair flowing over the shoulder of Hel's living side was a fiery golden-red.

CHAPTER TWELVE

I INTRODUCED HEL TO mead to celebrate our victory, and the days just after Loki defeated Frigg and saved us from permanent separation were a bit of a blur. A glorious, sensual, exhausting blur. It was just me and the woman I loved, and I could damn well get used to it.

I smiled, feeling better than I'd felt in, well, ever. We were eating dinner outside, on a high porch in Hel's castle. The setting sun had taken on its strange blue glow, making Hel's face look even more ethereal. We were in a public part of the castle, where we could be overseen, so she wore her illusion. But even that, it seemed, had softened somewhat. The living side of her face was different, fuller and gentler, more like the face she wore beneath the illusion.

Motherhood might suit her. The thought surprised me, but only for a heartbeat. I'd been toying with the idea of marriage, if I could only find the right way to phrase it so no one would think I wanted her kingdom. Why not children, sometime after that?

The children of Baldr and Hel would be glorious, after all.

"You're smiling," she said, putting down her goblet.

"You make me smile."

She raised an eyebrow and opened her mouth.

"Hel! Baldr!" Vigdis crashed through the door, making me jump in my seat. "I'm so sorry," she panted, "but we have a visitor. A *living* visitor."

"Vigdis, it can wait," Hel said, her voice sharp as the knives on our table.

"He's—I'm sorry, my Queen, he's quite insistent."

A dark figure loomed in the doorway behind Vigdis. I was on my feet before my brain could process what was happening, one of the dinner knives clenched in my fist. If this was a threat, I'd go down fighting to protect Hel.

My brother, Thor Óðinnsen, stepped through the door.

Vigdis cowered as he walked toward us, his unbeatable hammer Mjölnir glinting in the thick evening light. Hel's chair scraped the floor as she came to her feet.

"What are you doing here?" I yelled.

"Brother!" Thor boomed. "I've traveled far so we may drink together!"

He spread his arms wide, showing he held no weapons, and my shoulders relaxed. I stood, slipping the knife back onto the table.

"You traveled to Niflhel to say hi?" I asked.

Thor wrapped his arms around my chest and thumped me on the back. "Little brother, it would take more than death to stop me!"

"You're crazy as usual," I said, trying to stop grinning like a maniac.

Thor rumpled my hair and turned to Hel. He didn't flinch, of course; nothing scared Thor the Thunderer. "You must be Queen Hel?" he said, offering a dramatic bow.

Hel frowned. "Thor? Son of Óðinn?"

Thor grinned and took her living hand in his, pressing it to his lips. "The one and only, m'Lady."

Hel's living cheek flushed pink, and a little pang of jealousy tugged at my chest. She couldn't possibly be attracted to my idiot brother, could she?

"What in the Nine Realms are you doing here?" I asked.

Thor grabbed my flagon of mead and downed it. Then he grabbed Hel's and downed it too. "Can't wait to tell you," he said. "Let's eat! Where's the rest of the meal?"

Hel nodded at Vignis, who hurried through the door.

"It's on the way," she said. "Please. State your business."

Thor wiped his mouth on his sleeve and turned to me. "First, Baldr, tell me why you stayed. Frigg says one thing. But Hermod was here too, and his story's different. So what's the deal?"

I leaned back and crossed my hands behind my head, smiling as Thor polished off the entire poached salmon Hel and I were going to share. "And what, pray tell, are they saying?"

Thor ripped a chunk of bread off our loaf and bit into it, looking thoughtful. "Well, Frigg says you've been chained to a bed and forced to be a sex slave for the insane nymphomaniac Queen running this realm."

Hel raised her eyebrow.

Thor smiled at her. "No offense, of course," he said.

"None taken," she muttered.

"And Hermod?" I asked. Hermod was our youngest brother. I could scarcely believe he'd found the spine to openly contradict Frigg.

Thor belched. "Yeah, I had to get him pretty drunk. But, right before he blacked out, he said you actually wanted to stay here. Said you had a thing going with the queen here."

Vignis staggered through the doorway under an enormous plate of steaks, potatoes, and barrels of mead. I jumped up and took the platter from her, setting it in front of Thor. He drank the first barrel of mead without taking a single breath, then stared at me with all the subtlety of his infamous hammer.

"So? Which is it?" Thor asked.

"Which do you think?" I said, raising my arms and showing him my wrists. "Do you see any chains?"

Thor roared with laugher and smacked me across the back. "Damn! Hey, good for you, Baldr!"

Then he leaned across the table and smacked Hel's shoulder too. "And good for you, Queenie! Seducing Baldr the Beauty, huh? You must be more impressive under that dress than you look!"

Hel blinked, opened her mouth, and then closed it again. Thor didn't seem to notice. He downed another barrel of mead, tossed it off the balcony, and stared at the shimmering blue sky until we heard the sharp crack of wooden staves splitting against the stones of the courtyard. I winced. Hel crossed her arms over her chest and looked bored, as if having my brother blunder into her castle and start breaking shit was an everyday occurrence.

"Hey, that's not the only reason I'm here," Thor whispered. "Can we talk freely here?"

"Sure," I said.

Thor rubbed his beard, looking a little lost. "Listen, uh, Frigg's not happy about this whole arrangement. Loki's taking most of the heat, at the moment—"

"Loki?" I asked.

Thor stared at me like I was the biggest idiot in the Realms. "Brother, you do know Loki made the dart that killed you?"

"Oh. I thought it was an accident?"

Thor snorted and reached for a third barrel of mead. "Loki said it was an accident. But you know we all trust him about as far as we can throw him."

I glanced from my brother's mead-flushed cheeks to Hel. She looked pale.

"Did you know?" I whispered.

She shook her head, her living eye wide. I took her hand and kissed it.

"Then I suppose I'll have to thank Loki," I said, watching her cheek color.

Thor laughed again. "You know, I never did get you, Baldr. You got strange tastes. Strange! But listen, that's not the message I've gotta deliver."

"Wait, you're here officially?" I said. "I mean, you're actually delivering a message from the court of Asgard?"

Thor finished off the last barrel of mead and raised his eyebrows. "Yeah, course. Why the fuck not? You're not around anymore, Beautiful."

I brought my hand to my mouth to cover my smile. "Thor the Diplomat," I managed to say without cracking up.

Thor bowed his head. "Why thank you. And I'm here to tell you Frigg's pissed as shit, and she's cutting off all relations with this realm."

Hel and I stared at each other as Thor devoured the mound of potatoes.

"Niflhel doesn't have relations with Asgard," Hel said. "In all my years as Queen, I've never once been invited to Óðinn's council."

"That's what I'm saying," said Thor. "No relations."

Hel frowned, her brow furrowing. "Fine. We will not attempt to establish diplomatic ties with Asgard. You have my word."

"And don't try to start any fights either, because Óðinn's warriors will mop the floor with your dead cowards. From this point on, Niflhel is an enemy of Asgard."

"Understood," Hel said.

Thor smiled, belched, and pushed back from the table. "Good. Good work, all."

I stood up with him, and Thor pulled me into an embrace. "Brother! Good food here, you know. Mead's not half bad. You could've done worse."

I grinned. "I know."

"You two should come up to Asgard sometime. Visit me an' Sif. The boys'd love it. I tell you, Baldr, you won't believe how big they're getting. Strong, too."

"Didn't you just say we're now the enemies of Asgard?" Hel asked, her tone mild and friendly.

Thor frowned. "Oh. Yeah. I meant after, you know. Once all this blows over."

I clapped him on the back. "Thanks, brother. We'll keep it in mind. You take care."

"You too," he said, turning to Hel. "Listen. You be good to my baby brother, you hear?"

"Of course," she said, her face as stoic and serious as when she'd sworn not to start a war with Asgard.

I hugged him one more time before he staggered off the porch with Vignis, who was promising she'd taken very good care of his goats and his chariot. And yes, she remembered where they were.

"Well," Hel muttered under her breath, "that was the single most offensive diplomatic visit I've ever had."

I laughed. "Thor the Diplomat. He'll learn. I mean, he's got nowhere to go but up, right?"

Hel raised her eyebrow. "Are you sure you're actually related to that oaf?"

I pulled her into my arms, kissing her neck. "Oh, my love, you can't choose your family."

Family. Shit.

"Loki," I said.

Hel's eyes widened. "Where did that come from?"

"Shouldn't we talk to him?"

"Talk to him? Why?"

"If he's taking the blame for this, maybe we should offer to help."

Hel shook her head. "My father doesn't accept help. From anyone."

"Well, we could at least tell him we appreciate what he did."

She frowned. Hel never spoke of her parents, or her childhood, but I got the distinct impression it was not happy. "I don't know. You really think he'd want to talk to us?"

I shrugged. "Honestly, I'm not sure."

Loki had lived among the Æsir for ages, but he was still a big damn mystery as far as I was concerned. And usually he was an asshole, too.

"But he did do us quite the favor," I said. "And hey, if we're being cut off from Asgard, it's not like it can make matters worse."

WE RETURNED TO THE subterranean pool that night.

"Father," Hel said as the torches gleamed orange off the black water of the pool. "I wish to speak with you."

Her words echoed off the walls. The room fell silent. The inky pool seemed to swallow sound. Hel frowned and shifted on her feet.

"Father," she said again, louder this time. "I wish to speak with you."

A small gust of wind filled the room, making the torches flicker and flare. Then that too died down, and the room was again still, silent, and cold.

"That's odd," she said. "It's always worked before."

"Maybe he doesn't want to be bothered," I said. "Oh, well. At least we tried."

Another gust filled the room with frigid air. Waves surged and climbed out of the black pool. The water flashed opalescent, and Loki appeared.

He was hunched over, his face pale and his hair matted. His clothes were ripped and filthy, streaked with something I really hoped was mud. He pulled himself upright when he saw us, sweeping his hair from his eyes.

"Daughter. You called?"

Hel's mouth gaped open. "Father, are you hurt? Do you need help?"

Loki gave a sharp, hollow laugh. "From you? Are you kidding?"

Hel's face hardened. I stepped forward.

"Loki," I said. "We owe your our gratitude. The Æsir can't have been too pleased."

He winced. "You could say that."

"Is there anything we can do to help?" I asked.

Loki waved his hand in the air. "No, no, they'll get over it. No problems here. Just... no more favors?"

"Of course," I said. "We only wanted to thank you."

Loki ran his fingers through his hair and nodded. "Right. Yeah, no problems. And, Baldr..." For a second he looked as though he had more to say, but then he glanced over his shoulder and the moment passed.

"If that's all, I really should be going," he said.

Hel nodded stiffly. "Thank you, Father."

"I'd like to ask for your daughter's hand in marriage," I blurted out. I hadn't planned to say anything, but suddenly it seemed like the right time.

Loki's eyes opened wide. "Ah. Interesting. Well, I'd never presume to choose Hel's husband for her. Ask her yourself, pretty boy."

My heart did a funny little somersault as I turned to Hel. She held her hand over her open mouth, and her eyes glistened. Her illusion had vanished; I really hoped that was a good sign.

"I'm not trying to take your crown," I said, falling to my knees on the cold, damp ground. "I don't want your kingdom. I just want to be more than your consort."

She nodded. "Baldr, I—"

Loki coughed, and I turned to see him looking over his shoulder again. "Sorry to interrupt, kids, but I've got to go." He gave us a smile that didn't reach his eyes. "Make each other happy, okay?"

"Father, wait!"

Hel reached for him as the torches flared, and he vanished. The pool lapped quietly as I came to my feet, brushing off my pants. Hel frowned at the still waters where her father had just disappeared.

"You okay?" I asked.

She hesitated, pressing her lips together. "We've never exactly been close, but...Did my father seem odd to you?"

I laughed as I wrapped my arms around her waist. "Loki's always odd. There's a reason he's called the Lie-smith."

Her eyes drifted back to the dark pool. I trailed my fingers along the curve of her cheek. "He's Loki, my love. I'm sure he'll be just fine. Besides, it'll be good for the Æsir to solve this one on their own, without Baldr the Babysitter."

She sighed in my arms. "Yeah. You're right."

"And you still haven't answered my question," I said, running my hand down her back.

Hel smiled. "So Baldr Óðinnsen wants to be king of Niflhel?"

"No. I want to be your king."

"You would look very good in a crown," she said, twining her fingers in my hair.

I snorted. "I don't care how I look."

My voice trailed off as I realized how true that was. My appearance was completely irrelevant. For the first time in my existence, I had no agenda to further, no squabbles to smooth over, no role to fill the keep the Nine Realms humming. For better or for worse, I was forever beyond the reach of Óðinn's rewards and punishments.

I was free.

"Hel," I asked, meeting her eyes, "do you think you could cast an illusion on me?"

Her forehead furrowed. "What? Why?"

I wrapped my arms around her waist, loving this sudden, mad idea. "So we match, of course! Could you make me look like you?"

"I don't know. I guess I could try. But, why?"

I laughed. "Because I'm tired of being Baldr the Beautiful, damn it! Let's begin again, my love. Let me start over as Baldr, just Baldr, humble consort to Queen Hel."

"Husband," she whispered, with a smile. "Husband to Queen Hel."

EXCERPT FROM The Trickster's Lover[1]

THE *Sem Guði Hátíð* was slow going as my two windows rattled in their panes and cold rain streaked the glass. The lights flickered but stayed on; Chicago knew how to handle a storm. The only dictionary I'd managed to find translated Icelandic into French, so I had a second dictionary to translate the French into English. Some of the dictionary entries were supremely unhelpful, offering that the translation for the French preposition "de" could be "of, to, from, by, with, than, at, off," and, under some circumstances, "out of."

There were familiar characters in the *Sem Guði Hátíð*, like Óðinn, Thor, and Loki, but there was also plenty of ambiguity. Haf, for instance. According to my Icelandic-to-French dictionary, this meant "ocean," but was this the actual ocean? Was it the name of the god of the ocean? Or was it meant as a description, an attempt to evoke the vast size of the feast hall? Sometimes I was almost certain I'd understood a full sentence, but mostly it was like feeling my way through an unfamiliar room with the lights turned off.

It was fascinating.

I told myself I'd only work until midnight. When midnight came I made another cup of tea and said I would only work until one in the

---

1. https://payhip.com/b/ZuW8

morning. Now the clock above my tiny half-oven blinked quarter to two, and I ignored it.

"Girnud," I muttered to myself, trying out the words. I rolled them on my tongue, imagining Viking ships and longhouses, imagining woodsmoke, the spray of salt from the ocean.

"Girnud, löngun."

And then I was no longer alone in my apartment.

There was, perhaps, a crackle of electricity in the air, a quick gust of cold on the back of my neck, like a melting snowflake.

I looked up from the table. There was a very tall man standing in the middle of my apartment. I stood and stumbled backward, bumping awkwardly against the wall. Our eyes met, and my breath caught in my throat. He was unreasonably attractive.

"Uh, hi?" I stammered, staring at his full lips and long, fiery red hair.

He smiled, and my heart surged. *Damn, what a smile.* I fought the insane urge to smile back and tore my eyes off him, glancing at the door to my apartment. It was still closed, bolted, with the chain drawn. *How did...?*

I turned back to him, and he moved a step closer. He wore strange clothes; they looked like leather, black with streaks of gold and red, with an enormous cloak rippling behind him. His fingers were delicate, and his ice-blue eyes seemed to be laughing. He bent toward me, so close our lips were almost touching. So close I could smell him. Woodsmoke. Salt spray. Cold, and leather.

"Hello," he whispered, his breath warm on my neck.

My skin prickled, and I trembled as my body flushed with heat. I swallowed and tried to think. *It's the middle of the night,* I told myself. *And there's a strange man in your apartment.* I turned to face him, my gaze lingering on the soft curves of his full lips, wondering how they would feel—

I shook my head to stop myself. *You should not be thinking about kissing him.*

"What are you—" The words died in my throat as a jolt of recognition surged through my body. *I know you,* I thought. *I've been reading about you since I was thirteen.*

"Loki?" I whispered, my voice sounding very small. "Loki... of the Æsir?"

His eyes danced. "Very good. I am Loki, son of Laufeyiar." He gave me another slow, incendiary smile. "And right now, I'm admiring you."

The room suddenly felt very warm. I took a deep breath. "That's not possible," I whispered.

He tilted his head to one side and raised an eyebrow. "What's not possible?"

Neither of those things are possible.

*Find **The Trickster's Lover** at a wide selection of online retailers!*

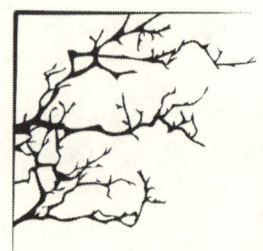

MORE FROM SAMANTHA MACLEOD

THE LOKI SERIES: URBAN Fantasy Romance inspired by Norse Mythology
The Trickster's Lover[1]
Honeymoon[2]
The Trickster's Song (TBD)

EROTIC SHORT STORIES
Persephone Remembers the Pomegranates[3] (free!)
Claiming Thor's Hammer[4]
Winning Freyja's Cloak
Tam Lin[5]

---

1. https://payhip.com/b/ZuW8
2. https://payhip.com/b/Z0Aw
3. https://payhip.com/b/YdbM
4. https://payhip.com/b/XMfK
5. http://www.subscribepage.com/u0p4g7

URBAN FANTASY & FANTASY Romance

Hel's Lover[6] (fantasy romance inspired by Norse myth)
The Night Watch[7] (M/M/M/F fantasy romance)
The Wolf's Lover[8] (urban fantasy romance)

---

6. https://payhip.com/b/Z7nb
7. https://lessthanthreepress.com/books/index.php?main_page=product_bookx_info&products_id=1446
8. https://payhip.com/b/03GE

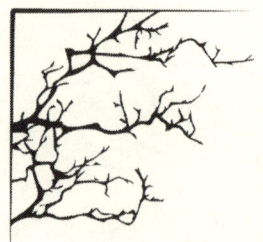

THANK YOU

YOU'RE AMAZING!

Thank you so much for reading independent artists. Without your support, I wouldn't be writing. So go out there and treat yourself to something special. You deserve it!

Now that you've finished Baldr and Hel's story, please do consider leaving a review. Reviews make or break the careers of independent authors like me, and I really do read every single one. I promise!

CLAIM YOUR FREE STORY

A sexy prince, an unforgiving enchantement, and a bargain with the fey...

SIGN-UP FOR SAMANTHA'S NEWSLETER AND RECEIVE A *free* EROTIC SHORT STORY!

Click here to claim your free story: http://www.subscribepage.com/u0p4g7

ACKNOWLEDGEMENTS

THIS MAY BE A LITTLE book, but it wouldn't have happened without a lot of help!

First, as always, I'm so thankful to my primary beta reader, my wonderful husband, who patiently waded through the first versions of this story and pointed out (gently, of course) the parts that weren't working.

Speaking of beta readers, thanks go out to Cate at The Book Medic and Jayne Ingram-Shover, who were both incredibly helpful.

Teresa Conner made the cover look gorgeous. Thank you!

Danielle at Caldwell Publishing and Tina at A Reader's Review Blog both made me feel like I should probably keep writing. Thanks, my friends.

Since publishing *The Trickster's Lover*, I've been lucky enough to connect with an amazing group of professionals. Bronwyn Green, Mira Stanley, Terrance Sené, and Janine Ashbless have given me more encouragement, advice, and support than I could ever repay. You ladies are the best! (They're also fabulous writers, and you should check them all out.)

And finally, thanks to my mom. When I finally told her I'm publishing erotica, she shrugged and said someday she'll tell me her college stories.

Mom, you're awesome.

Made in the USA
Columbia, SC
15 October 2024